THE DRIFTER IN THE WIND

DANIEL GRABOWSKI

Marie,
thank you for taking a chance on Jesse — I hope he doesn't disappoint!
Sincerely,

Copyright © 2022 by Daniel Grabowski

Published by DS Productions

All rights reserved.

This book may not be duplicated in any way without the express written consent of the publisher, except in the form of brief excerpts or quotations for the purposes of review.

The information contained herein is for the personal use of the reader and may not be incorporated in any commercial programs or other books, databases, or any kind of software without written consent of the publisher or author. Making copies of this book or any portion of it, for any purpose is a violation of United States copyright laws.

This is a work of fiction. Names, characters, places, and incidents either are the product of the author's imagination or are used fictitiously. Any resemblance to actual persons, living or dead, events, or locales is entirely coincidental.

ISBN: 9798373527101

❀ Created with Vellum

1

FISH OR CUT BAIT

Jesse Clayton stopped his horse when he saw the old man hit the ground. The trouble was a few yards ahead on the trail; a wagon held up by two men on horseback was what he made of it. Sure enough, their eyes found him, and he was part of this now. He tugged at the reins of his mare.

Getting closer, he could see the problem much clearer: atop the wagon sat a woman, not much younger than himself, doing an admirable job of hiding her fear. The old man was sprawled in the muck, his forehead all bloody, while a man in a ragged duster stood over him. Another, in matching attire, sat sentinel on his horse, his shotgun now aiming at Jesse.

"Just a conversation, mister," said the man standing. "You go on and git now."

"That's right, go on." The mounted one waved his shotgun as he spoke.

"This doesn't look like much of a conversation," Jesse said. He kept his voice low and cool, almost playful. "You got this poor feller lying in mud and his own blood, and you're pointing a gun at his lady. What kinda talking you doing here, friends?"

"The kind that's none o' your business," the standing man said.

For a moment, Jesse locked gazes with the woman. Her eyes pleaded with him. "Guess I'm making it my business, friend." Jesse pulled his town coat away from his hip and let his hand hover near his holster. He was cold and he was tired, but he'd be damned if he was going to leave that woman to her fate. "What's your names, boys?"

The man on foot answered: "Name's Dustin. On the horse is my brother, George."

Dustin's hand had gotten awful close to his hip. George's grip on that shotgun had gotten a little tighter, too.

"Well, my name's Jesse. Now that we're all well met, let's the three of us have a conversation. Nice and civil. Way I see it, you boys have two choices: first, y'all get back on your horses and ride off, and we all have a lovely evening. Second . . ." Jesse nodded toward his hip. ". . . you see where my hand is right now? If it gets any lower, it's gonna come back up a lot faster. I'll bet you're thinking 'but fast enough to plug us both?' Maybe. Maybe not. But I'm sure as day followin' night that I'll get you, Dustin, before either of you get me. So what'll it be boys?"

The brothers shared a glance. A long moment passed between them all, interspersed by the grunts of the old man. Jesse saw the temptation scrawled across their faces. Dustin's hand was twitching. George held that shotgun of his so tight it could've snapped in two. Jesse was suddenly aware of the sweat beading around the brim of his hat.

"Well, gentlemen?" Jesse said. "We gonna fish or cut bait?"

Dustin held firm for a moment as he eyeballed Jesse. Then he folded his arms and sighed. "Put your gun down, George," Dustin said. He drove a boot into the side of the old man before stepping away and mounting his horse. He tipped his scuffed hat to Jesse and the lady and waved his brother on. Their horses kicked up dust and dirt in their wake. Jesse kept his eyes on the two of them until he was of a mind that they were not about to change theirs. Once they were out of sight, he let out a long breath, pulled out his handkerchief, and gave his forehead a wipe.

He hopped down from his horse and greeted the lady with a "ma'am" and a tip of his hat. Then he knelt beside the old-timer and hauled him up into a sitting position. Half his face was slick with crimson from a deep gouge in his forehead. Jesse asked him if he was okay, and the man only moaned in response. Behind him, the woman jumped down from the wagon.

"Daddy! Daddy, are you okay?" She dabbed his forehead with a handkerchief, and the old man grunted in pain.

"Yeah, I'm . . . I'm fine, Winona. They didn't hurt you none?"

"No, Daddy, thanks to the kindness of this stranger." She looked at Jesse and smiled.

He believed it was pretty enough to disarm a man. She said something else, but Jesse didn't quite catch it, being lost in his own mind.

"Hey!"

That brought him back to the moment.

"You think you can quit daydreamin' and help me get him on the wagon?"

"Sure, ma'am." The pair of them heaved the old man up to his feet and walked him over to the back of the wagon.

"And don't call me ma'am. Name's Winona, Winona Squires. This is my daddy, Bill."

"Yes, ma'am." Jesse winced at his immediate mistake. "Sorry. Nice to meet you, Winona."

It took them about half an hour to get back to the ranch. Winona rode on the wagon with her father while Jesse followed on his horse. He noted that the fences had their breaks and holes that needed maintenance, and the cattle looked a little on the thin side even to him, who was no expert.

The house itself was big, if a little modest on the inside, with few furnishings beyond a wooden table and a few cabinets. Winona fed another log to the fire in the fireplace.

Suddenly, Bill yelled, "Sonofabitch!"

"Sorry about that," Jesse said. "But this wound needs cleaning. It ain't deep, but it's enough to cause trouble if you go and get an infection." He upended the bottle of whiskey on the cloth and then dabbed the wound again. Bill howled and pulled away.

"Why don't you let me worry about that and you pour us a drink?" Bill said. He pressed the cloth to his head and turned to Winona. "Baby, get us some glasses for the whiskey." Winona nodded and fetched them, returning to the table. Jesse poured them all a drink. Bill raised his and said: "To the kindness of strangers."

The three of them drank.

"You're too kind." Jesse said.

"Not at all. Last thing I remember is expecting death and fearing for my daughter. Here I am now sharing a drink with the man who prevented the terrible things my mind had conjured up." Bill grabbed the bottle and poured another round. "What brought you down to this part of Idaho anyhow, Mr. Clayton?"

"Just passing through."

"So, you're a transient?" Bill chuckled.

"More of a wanderer, but you could swing it that way, yes," Jesse said.

"Oh, don't mind him. He's all kinds of rude after a bang to the head," Winona said. "There anywhere in particular you're wandering to?" She'd gotten hold of some bandages now and was readying to dress her father's wound.

Jesse shrugged. "Wherever the wind takes me, I guess."

"Well, thank the Lord for the way of the wind this night. Anything I can do to repay you? Room for the night is the least of it," Bill said.

"That's awful kind, thank you. I could use some supplies, too, if you can point me to the nearest town." Jesse said.

"Won't be much there, but I can take you into Fortune in the morning. You'll be able to get a thing or two there from Wilkerson if he's around." Bill reached for the bottle and went to fill Jesse's glass. He shook his head, and the old man filled his own. Jesse's vision had started to wobble, and his mind felt locked away somewhere outside of himself. His limbs felt borrowed from another man, and his eyelids had become heavy as lead.

"Much obliged. Now, I'm struggling to wrestle my eyes open. If you two will excuse me, I think I'll go get some rest."

"Sure thing. Up the stairs, room on the left's all yours."

Jesse got up and pushed his chair under. He plucked his Stetson from the table and made his way up. Each step creaked underfoot.

Winona's voice came from behind him. "Why did you stop?" she asked.

Halfway up, he turned back to see her at the bottom of the stairs. "I did what anyone would do."

She shook her head. "Not around here. People just up and hide the moment there's trouble. But not you. Even seeing it was two to one, you kept on, laughing and talking at them like it was a game."

"That's what you thought? It was a game?" He leaned against the handrail. "You keep a secret?"

Jesse pulled his Colt from its holster with the swiftness of a viper. He tossed her the weapon, and she caught the heavy smoke wagon. He watched her hold it like she knew something wasn't right with it. As she inspected it, the realization spread across her face. She looked up at Jesse, who shot her the widest grin.

"There any place I can buy bullets in Fortune?"

2

GOD DIDN'T LEAVE, HE WAS DRIVEN OUT

The ride into Fortune wasn't long. The town sat across the edge of a huge pine forest, away from the plains where Bill's ranch lay. Jesse enjoyed the sight of the verdant pines that stretched for miles, even halfway up the mountain in the distance.

As the wagon rode into town however, the views turned much bleaker. Jesse took note of the houses left empty or boarded up, barns and stables that bore no signs of livestock, and the main strip itself that seemed rather devoid of activity.

"This what you meant when you said there wasn't much?" Jesse asked Bill next to him.

The old man scratched at his bandage. "Yup. Fortune ain't had much in the way of its name since the gold dried up a couple years back. Folks been up and sellin'. Even more so since the trouble with Cullen and his boys."

"Cullen?"

"Slim Joe Cullen. You chased off two of his gang, the Foy twins, last night. They been makin' lives hell for anyone fool enough to stick it out in these parts. Most have taken the mayor up on his offer and gone."

They passed a wagon on the other side of the road with a man loading wares into the back of it. Jesse had seen fewer wrinkles in leather than he saw on this man's face.

"You sell up to Mayor Crane, Jeremiah?" Bill called to the man as they passed.

"I did," Jeremiah said.

Bill stopped the wagon. "And just how much did he pay you?" he asked.

"Enough to start over some place new." Jeremiah spat a wad of brown into the mud. "Away from this sorry town."

"It's just on its knees is all." Bill pulled on the reins and the wagon jerked forward.

"This town is dead, Bill Squires!" Jeremiah squawked back. "It just won't admit it! God's left this place, so I'm off, too! And so should you!"

Bill didn't even bother turning his head as he replied, "God didn't leave, He was driven out. But He'll come back. Once we rid ourselves of Cullen and his rats!" He lowered the volume to say to Jesse, "That was Jeremiah Sims. Can't say I'm surprised to see him go."

Up ahead was the hotel, outside of which Jesse made out three figures, one dressed much better than the others.

"See the big feller with the cane and the fancy suit outside the hotel?" Bill said. "That's Mayor Crane. Since the gold mine ran empty, he's been buying up all the land around here and helping folks start again elsewhere. Why? I don't know. Has more money'n sense, that man."

Jesse saw Crane, and Crane saw him. He touched the brim of his Stetson, and Crane raised his cane as the wagon trundled by. At first glance, Crane didn't strike Jesse as a man without much sense. He dressed well and carried himself even better, by the looks of things. The two armed men, one on either side of him, were probably on his payroll, too—not the custom of a man without much in the way of brains, Jesse surmised.

"Has he offered to buy *you* out?" Jesse asked.

"Yup. Both times he fell well short of the valuation. The man forgets that failing gold mines and a town fulla outlaws don't much stop people's need for milk and cheese."

Bill stopped outside a saloon with an old sign that read 'The Jewel.' The joint's paint was peeling, and the faded wood housed a few bullet holes. "You hop off here with Winona. She'll look after you. I gotta deliver this dairy," Bill said.

Jesse shook the man's hand then he and the rancher's daughter got off the wagon.

Winona pushed through the swinging doors and Jesse followed. The place was empty save for the scattered tables. There were women in corsets idling at the back and behind the bar, a man so large that Jesse wondered if his father had been a bear.

"Why are we here?" Jesse asked. "This don't look like the kinda place that sells bullets."

"Like my daddy said, you'll want Wilkerson for those. And if he ain't in town by now, he won't be 'tll tomorrow. Besides, you're gonna need a shave before anything else, Mr. Clayton. And nobody in town cuts a man better'n Christie."

Jesse put a hand to his beard, feeling thick and wild hair. He *had* been on the road for a while. Maybe Winona had a point.

"Right you are, Miss Squires," came a gravelly voice from above. "On both Mr. Wilkerson *and* Christie's skill with a blade." The man who made his way downstairs had a gait that was as assured as his charcoal pinstripe suit. His sideburns and French-style mustache were immaculately set on his worn face, and his hair was slick and black, streaked with silver. He extended a hand to Jesse. "Frank Balfour, proprietor of the Jewel. And you are?"

Jesse took Frank's hand and felt a firm squeeze that bordered on unnecessarily hard. Naturally, he reciprocated the force, much to Balfour's pained amusement.

"Jesse Clayton. Thank you for the welcome, Mr. Balfour," Jesse said.

"Please, call me Frank," he said and then yelled over his shoulder, "Christie! Get your ass out here now! Got a man needs a shave and some *company*!" He looked back at Jesse and winked as he said that last part.

At that, a woman came forward from the pack of girls. She had mousey hair and a corset that looked uncomfortably tight. As she got closer, he noticed a deep bruise on her left cheek.

"Just the shave, please," Jesse said.

The proprietor shrugged, wide-eyed. "But of course, what man wants a free place to put his pecker when he can settle for a shave?" Frank eyed Winona and then looked back to Jesse. "Perhaps a man has it better elsewhere?" he added with a smile.

Jesse moved over to Winona, who was rigid with discomfort.

"Look, this beard is thick, and I could be a while. How about you go book me a room at the hotel for the night, and then I'll meet you there for some food. That sound okay?" he said.

"Sure. And don't feel like you have to say no to Christie's company on my account."

Jesse laughed. "I'm sure she's quite the companion, but that's not the way I like to do things."

CHRISTIE KNEW how to use a blade, indeed; she'd cut away most of the defiant fuzz on Jesse's face without harm or discomfort. He sat back in a chair at the poker table, while Frank sat across from him, shuffling chips between the fingers of his left hand, his right hovering over a deck of cards.

"And that's the long and short of it, really," Frank said. Beneath the grit in his voice, there was a hint of an accent from across the Atlantic—Irish, Jesse guessed. "Slim Joe Cullen and his loathsome crew of bastards have been terrorizing this town for the past few months, chasing away anyone passing through and hounding and robbing us almost once a week."

"You don't have a marshal or sheriff? Round up a posse and deal with it?" Jesse asked as Christie scythed his jawline.

"We had a sheriff. Cullen blew out his kneecaps and then dragged him along behind his horse. You learn pretty quick to cooperate with a man like that, much as I'd like to end the son of a bitch." Frank leaned forward. "Think that might be something you'd be up to, friend?"

"I'm just passin' through."

"Like you passed the Foy twins last night?"

So, word travelled fast in Fortune. Jesse wasn't surprised, given the population wasn't too far from zero. Still, there was trouble afoot, and he got the sense that with Frank asking for help, having known him all of five minutes, he must be desperate. The longer he stayed in town, the greater the risk of being pulled into something he didn't like.

"Sorry, Frank, but this ain't my fight."

"I thought I might finally have gotten some luck." Frank said, shaking his head slowly. He slammed the chips down on the table in frustration. "These days it seems Fortune favors the dead and no one else."

"How so?"

"Even with all the Cullen trouble, the dead still get a good night's sleep."

"All done," Christie said, and Jesse was grateful for the change of subject. She wiped down his cheeks and he ran a hand across them, savoring the smoothness. She held up a mirror with a crack down its center.

Jesse almost didn't recognize himself. Looking upon the stranger in the mirror, he noticed the angular lines of his jaw, cheekbones now prominent again, and a sharp nose marred only by a slight dent in the bridge, courtesy of a drunken misunderstanding a long time back in New Mexico. His dark hair was tucked behind his ears but beginning to get unruly now, as it almost reached his shoulders. Still, he looked more akin to his twenty-five years of age now, and less like an old mountain man. He gave Christie his thanks as he got up from the chair.

"Fine job of a chin strap there, Christie. Now fetch us another bottle then piss off!" He slapped her behind as she left the table. He caught Jesse's disapproval. "Have to treat a whore properly, lest they get delusions of their position."

"That the same for the mark across her cheek?"

Frank growled a laugh and shuffled the deck of cards. "You like poker?"

Jesse flashed him a stiff smile as he sat himself back down. "I like takin' people's money."

3

MY TWO LEFT FEET

Jesse thumbed through the dollars again and then pocketed them as he left the Jewel. He made his way down the street to the hotel, where he was greeted by a short, lank-haired, clammy-looking man named Wallace Dalby, who claimed to be the owner.

"Your room is taken care of, Mr. Clayton. Miss Squires is waiting in the dining room," Dalby said, his voice a little too high for a man.

Jesse ventured into the dining room, feeling greasy for having conversed with Dalby. Still, he was hungry, a little light-headed from the whiskey and buoyed by the winnings he'd procured from Balfour. His mind and his mood soon leveled when he saw Winona sitting in the dining room. She was not alone. They hadn't spotted him yet, so he lingered a little, seeing if he could get a sense of what they were discussing.

"... No, Mr. Crane, I will not!"

"Come on now, Winona, listen. Your daddy's only getting older, and are you really going to be able to look after that big ranch all by your lonesome?"

"My daddy's just fine. He won't sell, and especially not for so little."

"It's a starting offer, is all, Winona. I can go higher. I just need you to talk Bill around."

"I ain't gonna flannel-mouth my daddy."

"My apologies. No need to jaw me. I'm just an old man trying to help a friend."

Jesse decided enough was enough and made himself known. He saw the tension rush from Winona's face as she caught sight of him, and he'd be a liar if he didn't confess it warmed his heart a little. Crane's fat head turned, and the mayor shot up mighty fast for a man with a belly as big as a barrel. The man was quicker than he looked, Jesse noted.

"Mr. Clayton, Sullivan Crane. It's a pleasure." Another damned handshake. Jesse just wanted some food. He gave the mayor a smile and sat himself down between them.

"What seems to be the problem between you two?" Jesse asked.

"Oh, nothing, really. I just got the wrong pig by the tail, is all," Crane said. The man's voice was deep; Jesse swore he could feel it in his chest. Crane boomed a laugh, and Jesse's pleasant smile faded.

"I was asking the lady," Jesse said, wiping the smile from Crane's face. "You all right, Winona?"

"Fine, Jesse. Just a bit of a heated disagreement is all."

"Indeed, Miss Squires is right! And, might I say, fine work you've done for this town already, Sheriff."

Jesse's head snapped around. "Excuse me?"

Crane's bushy eyebrows met across the bridge of his nose. "You're the sheriff, are you not? Sent from Rathdrum?"

"I think you may have a hold of the wrong pigtail again, Mr. Crane."

Embarrassed and apologetic, Sullivan Crane gathered himself and grabbed his cane. "As a gesture of reparation, may I invite the both of you to my estate tomorrow, for breakfast?"

Winona didn't appear to be abhorred by the idea. And to him, breakfast was breakfast. He wasn't one to turn down a meal. "Sure thing, Mr. Crane. That's mighty kind." he said.

The rotund mayor made his way to the exit, and his two bodyguards rose from their table in the corner to join him. In his hunger, Jesse had failed to spot them. He took off his hat and lay it in Crane's now-empty chair.

"Sorry about that, Jesse," Winona said.

"No need. Only one outta line was him, by my make of it."

"He just won't shut up about the ranch. How stupid can a man be insisting on buying up half a dead town?"

"If it's dead then why don't you just sell?"

"Shut up."

Jesse laughed and said, "You haven't eaten without me, have you? I'm famished."

JESSE PUT down his knife and fork and finished off his water. "If that's what you're wanting, to be on stage entertaining folks? Singing? Hell, I'll buy your train ticket."

"You would do that for *me*?"

"It's a matter of dollars, Winona. I've seen enough of this country to know you'll enjoy chasing that dream a lot more than milking half-starved cows."

"But what if I end up failing?"

Jesse frowned and shrugged. "You end up back here." Winona chewed on her bottom lip. Jesse spied her hand resting on the table, and he felt an impulse to hold it, but he kept still.

"I've never left this place."

"Maybe it's time you did."

"Would you come with me?" she asked and looked him right in the eyes. To Jesse, hers were pools of a deep shade of blue a man could drown in if he weren't careful. He pondered whether drowning would be so bad after all. His gaze wandered to the dark tumbles of her hair before he realized she'd asked him a question.

"I'm just passing through."

She nodded slowly and smiled weakly, "Wind's blowing you a different way, huh?"

"Something like that," he said as he reached for his hat. "Come on. Your daddy'll be waiting on you outside. We've been talking way too long."

In the street, the wagon, which was much less full than it was this morning, was waiting, with Bill sitting atop. He held the reins in one hand and a cigarette in the other. "That's a mighty-fine chinstrap you're sporting there, son."

"The shave was her idea."

"Good to hear she's lookin' after you. She's good at that," Bill said, then added to Winona, "Come on, let's go before the sun creeps down on us."

"Actually, Daddy, I think I'd rather stay with Jesse." she said. Her voice had taken on a childlike quality. Jesse surmised it to be a means to get her way with her father. He decided he'd play along. It was bound to be a more fun evening spent with her than enjoying the company of a bottle of whiskey at the bar or another round of poker.

Bill's eyes narrowed at her then shifted across to Jesse. "You'll look after her. No funny business?"

"You have my word, Bill. I'll behave."

"It ain't your behavior I'm worried about. She's apt to fight when she drinks." The old man chuckled, and Jesse wasn't completely sure he was joking. "Y'all have a good night." At that, he flicked the reins, and the wagon began to trundle off down the road.

Once the wagon was far enough away, Winona turned to him and said: "What do you wanna do?"

"I was thinking I might try to relieve Frank Balfour of some more of his money."

"I like poker. Can I play?"

"I dunno, *can* you?" Jesse couldn't resist the urge to poke fun. It clearly worked as Winona's hands found her hips.

"How about if I win a hand you dance with me?"

"That is a bet I will take, Miss Squires." He offered her his arm. "May I?"

Winona took his arm and together they walked across the mud and into the Jewel.

WITH THE COOL air of the evening behind them, the Jewel was a lot livelier than it had been when Jesse had gotten his shave from Christie. Beneath a haze of smoke rising to the ceiling, the air was hot and thick with the smell of whiskey and men in need of a bath.

Christie was now leading a man upstairs, while the other girls were entertaining men themselves presumably, as Jesse could not see them among the crowd. He estimated there was the better part of forty patrons in the Jewel. Among them he saw Sullivan Crane, flanked, oddly enough, not by his bodyguards but by two of Balfour's women. The piano was playing a cheerful melody which had many patrons dancing in spite of the odd janky note.

Jesse and Winona, arms still linked, made their way across the saloon and found themselves at a back table. They sat down and Jesse ran his fingers across the smooth green felt. The dealer asked what their choice was tonight and the two of them agreed on poker. The dealer dealt them each a hand, and as they checked and swapped out cards, the pair kept stealing glances at one another. Winona hadn't stopped smiling, and if he dared himself to check, Jesse Clayton imagined he might find one painted across his face, too.

Jesse bet a dollar and Winona raised two. Deciding to nip this in the bud, he called her bet. Her smile spread into a devilish grin as Jesse and the dealer both awaited the reveal. Sure enough, she laid down her five cards as she announced her hand:

"Three of a kind. Aces, Mr. Clayton."

Jesse looked down and spread the cards in his hand as he checked once more. He had both the two of hearts and the two of spades, along with three queens. He looked up at Winona and smiled then tossed his hand to the dealer.

"Looks like I owe you a dance, Miss Squires. If you don't mind, I'd like to have a drink first, on account of a need to loosen up my two left feet. I'm sure you understand."

The pair of them laughed as they moved their way through the jumble of people to the bar. Jesse ordered two whiskeys from the big bear that was Big Dan, who grunted as he poured. They downed their drinks and slammed the glasses on the table.

The sudden sound of gunfire came from outside.

The piano music jerked to a halt as everybody looked outside. Another shot. Two. Three. Riders on horses flashed by the saloon as still more shots rang out in the night.

As the sound of horses and gunfire faded away, a lone horse rode into view outside. Frank Balfour pushed his way through the crowd and through the saloon doors. "Sullivan!" he shouted from outside. Reluctantly, the fat mayor made his way out as well.

"Stay here," Jesse said to Winona. He left her at the bar and joined the two to see for himself.

The horse had stopped out front. The three men stood regarding it. There was a man tied behind it. His clothes and his body were a torn and bloody mess. He was unmoving.

"This was around its neck," Frank said and tossed it to the floor. It was a crude piece of wood with a star pinned to it. Written across the board in blood, long since dried were four words:

MEAT YOR NEW SHERIFF.

4

DON'T SHOOT

The joy and fervor for the evening had all but evaporated. The sight of a dead sheriff tended to do that to people.

With the help of Big Dan, Jesse and Frank had taken the body to the graveyard behind the church. Crane had followed, and Jesse was not sure why as he lugged the dead man across the road and into the yard full of gravestones.

Tucked away in the corner of the yard was a patchy space of green. It was here they settled the body. Dark was rolling in fast now, and in the torch light the three men took turns digging. Crane looked on, wringing his hands.

"Sullivan, what was his name? So I can tell the preacher in the morning," Frank said as he handed the shovel to Jesse. He stepped out of the hole and wiped his sleeve across his forehead.

"I have to confess that I do not know," came Crane's solemn reply. "The message I got from Rathdrum was that they were sending a man down. They never gave me a name."

Jesse shared a glance with Frank before he drove the spade into the ground again. The poor stranger had come to Fortune to help bring order. To have happened across the Cullen gang enroute was an uncanny irony not lost on Jesse. He hoped that when his time came that he would go in a slightly more dignified manner.

"Well, at least that'll save us time on a stone," Frank said. He turned to Jesse and added, "Stop there, Clayton. You go on and get." His attention moved to Big Dan. "You finish up here and take the morning off."

Big Dan nodded and heaved the deceased sheriff. He hurled the body into the grave so fast it almost caught Jesse as he climbed out. Jesse picked up his hat and made his way back through the gloom to the lights of Main Street and his room for the night.

KNOTS TIGHTENED like screws in Jesse's shoulders as he pushed through the door. He gritted his teeth at the pain. His eyes felt so heavy that for a moment he didn't register the lamplight, or the figure on his bed. His mind caught up with his eyes. and his hand snatched his Colt from the holster.

"You really are fast," said a familiar voice. And with that familiarity, he felt the tension rush away. The heaviness in his limbs felt unbearable.

"God damn, Winona. I could have shot you," Jesse said as he holstered his gun. He hung his hat and his jacket on a chair and sluggishly made his way to the bed where she sat.

"Not without any bullets you won't," Winona said. She moved over to let Jesse sit down, careful to hold her dress so he wouldn't sit on that, too.

"Good point." Jesse took off his gun belt and dumped it on the floor. It felt nice to get the weight of it off his hip. Not quite as nice as it was to have some company, mind. "Not to sound unappreciative of your presence, Winona, but what're you doing here?"

"I didn't want to ride home in the dark."

"A dead sheriff'll do that to ya."

"I figured you wouldn't mind, or you'd ride back with me."

"Sounds like you've got me pegged," he said and then immediately yawned. He stretched out to lie down. He felt almost every muscle cry out as he did; a few joints popped and crackled, too, for good measure.

"You want help with your boots?" Winona asked.

"I don't think either of us wanna deal with the smell," Jesse said. "It's been a long day, and tomorrow might could be, too."

"You leavin'?"

"Most likely."

"Oh." He could hear the sadness in her voice. It sent a tightness through his chest. "Where are you headed?"

"Wherever the—"

She cut him off. "Wind takes you, yeah. Spare me that crap, Jesse. Nobody just wanders. Everybody's going somewhere or after something."

Jesse pushed himself up onto his elbows. In the yellow light of the lamp, half of her shrouded in darkness, he felt the pull inside himself to tell her everything. About him and about his past. The things he'd done. The person he used to be.

If he did that, he'd be risking her life.

"I'm looking for someone." He settled on that. "Somebody who used to know my mother."

She leaned in closer to him now, captivated by his openness. "Who?" She asked and the hotness of her breath made him aware of how cool the room was. He wanted to reach out for her warmth.

He wasn't sure what it was about her that he found so attractive, when there was so much about her that was different from any woman he had known before: the women he crossed in the street, property of their husbands; the whores in every saloon he'd ever been in, property of any man that wanted them, if only for a little while; the few women he had dared get close to once upon a time, cruelly snatched away by the nature of his life back then.

And then there was Demi Barrett. Maybe that's what it was. Winona's strong will reminded him of Demi and—

Winona poked his arm. "I said who?"

She'd jabbed him hard, and he rubbed at the side of his arm as he tried to recall the who she was after. "Doesn't matter who, probably won't find 'em anyway. It's been a long time since I've seen 'em, even longer since I seen my mother. Still, gives me something to do to go lookin'."

"You could come with me. If I left that is. I don't much like the thought of travelling alone."

Jesse risked a hand on her back. She didn't flinch. She didn't move. He left if there, wondering if her skin would be as soft as her dress. There he was again, getting himself lost in his own head. Damn fool was tired and in the company of a woman who was stirring up feelings he wasn't sure he wanted stirred.

"You just want a bodyguard," Jesse teased.

"The hell I do!" Winona replied as she dug her hand between her breasts and pulled out a derringer. The little silver pistol with one barrel sitting atop the other looked almost comical in her hands, like a child's toy. He knew that it wasn't a plaything, and he'd bet she knew how to shoot it, too. Growing up on a ranch with a man like Bill Squires, what else was a girl to do?

"Hey, now, don't shoot," Jesse said as he lay back and put his hands up.

"Relax, cowboy," she said as she tucked the gun away. "Only people I'm fixin' to use it on is Cullen and his boys."

That gang. They were a problem. An outfit that treats a man like they did the sheriff before he'd even had the chance to piss them off was an outfit that was to be taken seriously. The sooner he was out of town the better. He'd get his bullets from the salesman when he came to town tomorrow and be gone.

But what about her? He watched her rearrange her dress, having finished hiding the derringer. Could he leave her now, knowing the kind of danger she would be in?

"Winona. That gang . . . you can't be messing with those people. You'll get yourself hurt, or worse."

"I'm not stupid, Jesse. But—"

"No. No buts, nothing. Trust me . . . I've come across people like this before. I've dealt with gangs like this before."

"You have?"

"Yeah." He hesitated. "I was a bounty hunter a time back. Brought in a few like these people." It wasn't a complete lie. He had been a bounty hunter, but the bounties he'd brought in weren't like these men. But he'd known men like it once upon a time. "Things in Fortune are bad right now, I know. But trust me, things'll get worse before they get better. And it'll get bloody before it gets done. Real bloody. You should get out of here before you get caught up in it."

Winona lay her head on the lumpy pillow next to him. "Sounds like you care about me."

"Maybe I do." He was grateful for the poor lighting as his cheeks felt warm. His heart felt like a locomotive gathering speed.

Her eyes searched his in the faltering light. She was waiting on him. He knew it. But he couldn't bring himself to move. He could lie to himself and say it was the tiredness, the aching in his muscles, preventing him.

"You haven't done this much before, have you?" she asked softly.

To Jesse, it sounded sympathetic to the point of pitying. She was reading him like a book. Nobody had ever done that to him before. He'd been careful to guard himself, keep people at arm's length. And yet, in one conversation, she'd dug more out of him than he'd shared with anyone in years. He thought about lying, but part of him knew she'd see right through it. Even in the dark.

"Never," he said with an undercurrent of shame.

Winona leaned over to him and planted her lips on his cheek.

"That's okay, Jesse. Goodnight." She turned over on the bed and Jesse watched the back of her head until the light faded completely.

5

THE DIFFICULT CHOICES

Everything ached. He'd woken up to every one of his muscles moaning in pain, chastising him for his endeavors yesterday. His head throbbed from the whiskey, too. Jesse turned away from the light pouring in from the window and saw Winona's face. He had forgotten she was here.

Her eyes were closed. He watched the steady rise and fall of her chest for a moment. He peeled himself off the bed gingerly—partly because he didn't want to wake her, but also because it was difficult to move without discomfort.

Jesse picked up his gun belt and put it on, careful again not to make a sound. He then grabbed his coat and his Stetson from the chair and, as he reached the door, took one last look at Winona. Her dark hair had fallen across her face, and now it fluttered with every exhale. He said a silent goodbye before slipping out of the room.

Outside, he felt the crisp cool air of the morning. Despite the sun's best efforts, summer's days were numbered, and the fall was beginning to get its hands on the weather. Not that Jesse minded; he'd prefer the chill of the breeze to the sweat from a hot day's riding. He looked up and down Main Street, looking for a wagon that might belong to the salesman Winona had mentioned. What was his name again? Wilkinson? Wilburton? Wil-something. Nevertheless, he saw nothing but a couple of early risers walking the street.

He cast his eyes across to the Jewel where he and the others had met the sheriff. Its doors were closed, but up on the balcony he spied Frank Balfour. He stood in his slightly yellowed long johns, leaning with a cup of coffee in his hand. His hair remained immaculate. Balfour's eyes roamed the street, too, until they came across Jesse, and the man raised his cup and tilted his head.

Jesse still wasn't sure what to make of Balfour. He'd given him a warm welcome to town and been respectful enough when his request for help had been turned down, and even more so when Jesse had taken his money. But a man who runs a saloon is not a man with the kindest of hearts. Not one had he come across that didn't have a vein of something sinister running through them. Balfour didn't cut the frame of a rotten man, but he was hiding something, Jesse was certain. Could he be in league with Cullen? It wouldn't be so far-fetched to be the brains behind the outfit.

He would know when the Jewel would be filled with people, plump and ready to be relieved of their dollars and valuables. It wouldn't be hard to get word to Cullen, then play the victim along with those actually hit by the robbers, before recovering any 'losses' and a nice cut of whatever the gang took on top of it. It was simple.

Simple plans were often the best.

Jesse returned the greeting with a tip of his hat. Balfour smiled, flung the dregs of his coffee into the street and then retreated inside, showing Jesse the cheeks of his ass through the open flap of his undies. God damn if he hadn't done that on purpose.

Jesse moved to step into the street when he was stopped by a voice.

"You Clayton?"

Jesse turned to see two men sitting on a bench outside the hotel. The one that had said his name was balding and heavily tanned. Jesse couldn't say much about his friend, whose face was hidden under the brim of his hat. Jesse could only catch the bristles of the edge of a greying beard, but there was a familiarity about the both of them that Jesse couldn't place. He'd seen them somewhere before, he knew that much; where, though, he couldn't recall.

"I am," Jesse said.

The pair of them stood up together. The silent one walked off and round the side of the hotel; the one that had spoken walked toward Jesse.

Jesse's hand waved over his hip.

"Easy now, partner. Name's Brad." Brad held his hands wide and away from himself. He wasn't looking to make himself a threat. "Me and my associate are in the employ of the mayor."

The bodyguards.

Jesse settled his hand and apologized. Of course, now he remembered. He also remembered the reason why they were most likely here. "You takin' me for some breakfast?"

"It was my understanding that I'd be picking up two," Brad said.

Jesse scratched at his chin, and then looked up to the window of the room he had been staying in, in which Winona now lay sleeping. "You'd be right in that assumption, but I think it'd be best if we let her sleep."

A carriage wheeled around from the side of the hotel and stopped in front of the two of them. Brad opened the door and then gestured for Jesse to get inside.

Jesse stepped in.

In his travels, Jesse Clayton had seen a lot of things. He had seen plenty of houses, ranches, farm steads and estates. Sullivan Crane's estate was something else entirely. They'd passed the entry gate what felt like miles ago, and as the carriage drove down a road bracketed by pines, he surmised it had been cut through a dense thicket, as trees were all he could see on either side. Even the sunlight struggled to make its way through. It felt like dusk was falling despite the fact it had yet to reach noon.

He was about to ask how long it would be when suddenly the

thicket ended, and Jesse was blinded by the sudden rush of light. He had to shield his eyes as the carriage slowed to a stop.

Still blinking, he got out and was struck by the majesty of the building before him. Big was an understatement. Steps led up to a huge set of carved oak doors. He counted six windows across the two floors. Pillars supported a balcony on the second floor, from which Crane waved to him.

"Good morning, Mr. Clayton. Brad, please bring him through and see him to the courtyard out back." At that, he disappeared.

"Quite something, ain't it?" Brad said. "It'll look even better once it's finished. Come on." Brad walked up the steps, and the huge doors opened at his approach. As Jesse stepped inside, he saw that it was not by magic but by two maids. The ladies did not make eye contact.

Inside, things were a little less impressive. Much of the work still needed to be done, as walls were being constructed and the ceiling had the beginnings of a painting in one corner. The foyer, the hallways, and the rooms they pased before leaving the back of the house all needed furnishing. The house was rather bare, hollow, in fact.

Brad waited at the door and told Jesse to go out into the courtyard and sit at the table that had been prepared. He did so, and a maid poured him a glass of water. She disappeared before he could thank her, and the huge presence of Sullivan Crane sat down across from him.

"Delighted you could make it, Mr. Clayton. But forgive me for asking about the whereabouts of Miss Squires. I believe I had invited her, too."

"She was a little busy, Mr. Crane, but she sends her apologies along with her warmest regards." Jesse smiled through the lie. Crane took it well enough.

"I must confess, I actually find it a little fortunate, this turn of events. Now we can talk as men, and not mind the fragility of a woman's disposition."

Jesse forced the smile a little longer; beneath it, his teeth gritted at the comment. "Fortunate indeed. What, may I ask, is it you wished to discuss that may upset a woman?"

Crane barked a laugh. "Come now, Jesse. I may call you Jesse, yes?" Upon getting approval, he continued. "Let us eat first. We have plenty of time to get to that. Over a cigar in my office, perhaps? In the meantime, when's the last time you had meat that wasn't dried?"

THE STEAK WAS JUICY. It was delicious. And so was the whiskey that went with it. Crane certainly had a taste for the finer things in life, and Jesse was grateful for the invitation. In the back of his mind a sliver of guilt itched. He'd make sure not to mention the steak to Winona. He surmised that would not go down too well.

They had moved on from the courtyard and upstairs into the mayor's office. Unlike the other rooms of the house downstairs, this one was very much complete. Two of the walls were lined with books. Another was lined with trophies from hunts—beasts of varying sizes, even a grizzly. Jesse doubted that Sullivan had brought these creatures down himself, but it didn't surprise him the man had the vanity to display them as such.

Crane sat behind a huge mahogany desk. He opened a box, took out two cigars, and offered one to Jesse, who shook his head. If he was to smoke, he'd roll a cigarette. He liked to draw it in deep and feel it burn in his lungs, not roll it around his mouth. Smoke tasted like smoke, no matter what it was that burned.

"If you won't smoke, you can at least take a seat," Crane said, nodding to the chair next to Jesse, who sat on it. "Let me tell you a story, Jesse. I came to this part of Idaho just shy of two years ago. I arrived in Fortune just as its . . . fortunes started to turn for the worse. You should have seen it. The gold mine pulled in men by the dozen to work it, and the town was booming with the trade of those passing through. Hundreds a week!

"But as I said, things turned for the worse when the mine dried up. It felt like overnight the people up and went with it. Oswald Mabin, the man who owned it, looked to up and get out quick. I offered to take it, and this house, too, the price being in my favor and all."

"Why would you take on an empty mine?"

"It isn't about the mine. It's about the land, son. Fortune is a lot like this house, you see. When I bought it, it was a mess. Mabin had started it and abandoned it when he'd first gotten wind of his mine drying up, I suspect. It was fortunate for me, however, as he hadn't gotten as far as barely finishing the foundations. It meant I could mold this house in my image. Really make it my *own*. Which is what I wish to do with Fortune. What I believe I can do with that town is leave my mark on it and create a lasting legacy. And it all starts with that mine for one reason."

Crane stared at Jesse for a moment, and he realized the mayor was expecting a response.

"Let me give you a hint, son." Crane chuckled, a deep rumbling that ended in a cough. "Look out the window, Jesse. What do you see?"

Jesse looked. All he could see were the pines.

"Those pines are this town's ticket to glory, son. Think about it. We're in the middle of a huge change in this great country. Many are making a wonderful pilgrimage as we all embark on a collective settling of the West. And what is everybody going to need when they need to build their homes, their wagons, their tools and their barns and their fences and whatever else?"

This time Jesse answered him. "Wood."

Crane jabbed a chubby finger at him. "Correct, my boy. And we are currently surrounded by some of the best quality pine in the whole of the United States. That old gold mine will be the beginnings of a sawmill. And once operation starts, Fortune will never be the same again."

"Then why are you trying to buy people out of their businesses and their homes? Surely if you're here to resurrect the town, they just need to hold on and soldier through it until you bring them all the good times you're promising."

Crane sighed. He crushed the remains of his cigar in the ashtray and then laced his fingers together on the desk. "It seems like them, you can't quite grasp the bigger picture here, my boy. But don't you worry, I'll explain it to you, and then I'll explain why I brought you here. I see you fitting into this vision I have, you see. I see you fitting in and prospering alongside me."

Alongside Sullivan Crane. Now there was a thought. If this wonderful speech was anything to go by (He clearly loved the sound of his own voice.), alongside him was not a place that Jesse fancied being. Nevertheless, that steak was mighty good. It wouldn't hurt to indulge the man a little longer.

"Prosper how?"

"Piqued your interest now, have I? Good." The word was drawn out almost like a growl. "With the town on its knees, businesses were going under. Some were more essential than others, I'll admit, and those did get more favorable prices. But I bought these properties and these businesses from people who no longer wished to be in Fortune and agreed on buy-to-let arrangements with those who wished to stay. Each one of those establishments was saved from oblivion. And they will be delivered into prosperity by my hand when my lumber yard is up and running."

Jesse thought that Crane would make a pretty good preacher, doing his best to sell himself as the selfless savior of Fortune. His vision was almost as grand as the décor in this room.

"That's all well and good, Sullivan. But where is it you see me falling into all this? I don't own a business and I have no mind to," Jesse said.

"What does any town need? It needs law and order, and somebody to be its righteous hand."

Jesse could not help but laugh. "You hear me talk off a few gun thugs and think I'm a law man? You're sadly mistaken, Sullivan."

"I'm no fool. I know you're a man who's likely been on the wrong side of the law more than he's been on the right. But that's the past." Sullivan rose from his chair and leaned over his desk. "I see a man to be *respected*." He prodded the table. "A man who will get things *done*." He prodded again. "Who isn't *afraid* to make the *difficult* choices."

One more time. "Is that not you . . . or am I sorely mistaken?" Sullivan let the question hang in the air as he stared at his would-be sheriff.

Jesse lowered his head, faking deference as he thought up the words to let the man down as gently as he could. He thought Sullivan Crane to be full of hot air and ballyhoo. But to phrase it that way might just make an enemy of him, and it was never wise to give a man with money a reason to dislike you.

"All right, you think on that while I pour us a drink," he heard Sullivan say.

As Jesse regarded the floorboards, he noticed something: a sliver of wood between a gap in the boards. He leaned over and worked it out of there with the tip of his thumbnail. He thought it could be a matchstick with its end broken off, but it felt different in a way he couldn't quite figure. He slipped the stick into his pocket and lifted his head again as he sensed Sullivan turning back around.

Jesse accepted the glass and took a sip of the bourbon, savoring the fierce burn of it as it hit the back of his throat. "I'm sorry, Sullivan. As nice as your bourbon is, I'm going to have to decline your offer of sheriff."

Crane's glass paused at his lips and his bushy gray eyebrows darted up. "Disappointing, my boy. Is the quality of my bourbon deserving of a reason why?"

Jesse swallowed down the last of his and grimaced at the heat all the way down to his stomach. Then he said, "You're not the first person in Fortune to ask for my help since I arrived here. I'll tell you what I told them. I am just passing through. I got somewhere to be, and this town's problems are just that—the town's. Not mine."

Sullivan drained his glass and then put it down on his considerable desk. He nodded his head slowly for a moment, mulling over what he'd just heard. Then he stood up fast and offered his hand to Jesse. "Very well. I appreciate your honesty."

The two men shook hands.

"Thank you for the food. And the bourbon."

"You're welcome, my boy. Thank you for the company. I'll see you at the Jewel this evening? A game of cards, perhaps?"

"Sure thing."

"Good. I'll see you later. I'll have Brad take you home."

"Thank you, Sullivan." Jesse was almost out the door when a thought occurred to him. He dipped back into the office and said, "Can I just ask: did you ever make an offer to Frank Balfour?"

"I did. He never accepted."

"Why?"

"He said the dope trade was far more valuable to him than any offer I could ever make."

6

IF I DON'T HAVE IT, YOU DON'T NEED IT!

A sheet of gray had been thrown over the sun, the kind of heavy and dark clouds that would have a betting man predicting rain. It was early evening when Brad dropped him off at the edge of town, the side with which Jesse was not familiar. This part had taken the worst of the economic slump. While Main Street still had the illusion of good health in its footfall and appearance, the signs of disrepair were clear here: houses left open and abandoned, one with no roof; a stable that was no longer in use; and a store, its front window long since broken.

None of these places were empty, though.

There were rough sleepers dwelling within the rundown structures. Mostly men, but Jesse could see the occasional woman. While a lot of them kept to themselves around a fire, or slept away their misery, there were a few that had noticed Jesse's presence as he walked down the muddy street. They watched him with glassy, vacant eyes. It may have appeared that he had their undivided attention, but it was likely that their minds were elsewhere. A place they frequented courtesy of Frank Balfour, perhaps.

No, he thought. It wasn't his problem. Yet again, Jesse needed to rid himself of the nascent thoughts of how he could involve himself in this town's issues. He would not discuss with Balfour his dope trade or if he knew Joe Cullen. He was going to get his damned bullets, retrieve his horse from Bill's ranch, and be done with the place. Fortune would be nothing but a memory.

But so would Winona.

The thought caught him off guard and he wasn't quite sure why it did. She was a lovely girl. But she had her plans, and he had his. That was that. He suddenly wished his horse were much closer. It'd be easier to just disappear and not have to say goodbye. Such a silly thing: he'd not known her more than a day.

Well, what did you expect, Jesse? She's the first woman you've had in your bed, even if she was fully clothed.

He rounded the corner back onto Main Street and was grateful for what he saw there. Not more than a hundred yards away was a wagon that had not been there the day before, with a huddle of people gathered around. Surely that was the salesman. He'd get his bullets and get out of Fortune.

He walked down Main Street, past the Jewel and the hotel, fortuitously not running into anyone familiar before he reached the wagon.

The man's name wasn't Wilkinson.

Emblazoned on the side of his wagon was *T. H. WILKERSON: SALESMAN EXTRAORDINARE*. "If I don't have it, you don't need it!" The painted gold words were drawn all fancy, and Jesse had to admit they looked nice against the navy-blue paint job. It looked a bit scuffed and dinged, with the odd chip in the paintwork here and there. Such was the nature of a travelling salesman, he guessed.

The group of people peeled away, each of them holding a bottle of something, looking plenty happy with themselves for having purchased it.

"I'm sorry, good sir. I'm afraid I am done for the day," Wilkerson said. His voice was refined to the point where it bore no sense of an accent to place the man's origin. It reminded Jesse of a British man he'd come across once upon a time. It sounded funny, pretentious, like he knew more than you and wanted you to know that.

"This'll just take a minute." Jesse said, stepping closer to Wilkerson. The salesman eyed him through his circular spectacles as he grabbed the chain hanging from his waistcoat. Out popped a silver pocket watch that he glanced at before nodding.

"See that it does . . . say . . ." Wilkerson said as his head lifted, and he adjusted his top hat. His lips pursed, making his whisper thin mustache and goatee look all the more ridiculous. "Your name wouldn't be Clayton, per chance?"

"It is." Jesse suddenly felt on edge.

"I have more than a minute for you. Frank Balfour promised half rates on Ellie Jane if I kept around until you showed up. I thought it to be a joke, honestly."

"Is that right?" Jesse said. Frank must have seen him ride out with Crane's boys and figured he'd be gone a while. A nice gesture, or was it the case that Jesse was a mite more useful with a Colt that wasn't empty?

"Now, it is my understanding, sir, that you are in the market for some firepower. Is that correct?"

"It is. I just need—"

"Say no more, my good man," Wilkerson said, ignoring him. He walked to the back of the wagon and waved Jesse with him. There was a small set of doors on the back. He opened both with a creak and then stood back. The man was carrying an arsenal. Inside was an array of pistols, shotguns, repeaters. Wilkerson had enough firepower to arm half the town.

"Here, take this," he said and handed Jesse a shotgun. It was about as long as his arm, a double barrel with a stained wooden stock. He couldn't help but have a look down its sights. "Now what you're holding there is a Cimarron Coach Gun. That right there is the 1878 model, beautiful craftsmanship. I will tell you this for nothing, sir, whatever it is you point and fire both barrels at, there will not be much left. It's American made so you can be assured of its quality, my good man. And *that* is a Wilkerson guarantee."

Jesse dry-fired the trigger and then popped the catch on the barrels. It was in pristine condition. "This is a fine weapon, Mr. Wilkerson but—"

"My goodness where are my manners?" Wilkerson said and tipped his hat. "Tobias Henry Wilkerson at your service." He plucked the coach gun from Jesse's hands and placed it back on its hooks. "Now, what about this?" He handed Jesse a beauty of a weapon. He knew it on sight: a Winchester lever-action rifle. The polished wood shined beautifully, and the iron-framed rifle felt light yet reassuring as Jesse nestled it into the crook of his shoulder. "Beauty, is she not? She's lightweight and low maintenance and she'll chamber almost anything: .44-40, .38-40. Hell, even .32-20. There is a reason why these rifles have been so popular for over a decade. If your Colt won't suffice, she'll get the job done, easy."

Jesse pumped the lever twice, the motion felt smooth, like an extension of himself. A fine piece of weaponry and in top condition. "I can imagine. I've used one before, but never owned my own."

"You could for thirty dollars."

Jesse handed it back promptly.

"Well, now, maybe the Cimarron for twelve?" Tobias said as if he could see the temptation written on Jesse's face. "Now, and I guarantee you this," he said as he put back the Winchester and then pointed a finger at Jesse. "You will not find a weapon in better condition than you will from me. I tell you that for free, sir."

"Maybe some other time. For now, I'm not after that kind of firepower."

"Then what are you interested in, friend? My miracle tonic?" Tobias circled his wagon again before Jesse could stop him and reached for a bottle on a shelf at the front of it. He brandished it at his would-be customer, and Jesse could see the dark, amber liquid within. It reminded him of urine . . . but thicker. "This is wonderful stuff, and I am running almost dry of it. Why, that crowd you saw upon your arrival? Almost cleaned me out! I imagine they'll come for the rest in the morning."

Jesse spied at least a dozen more bottles on the shelf, and if he recalled correctly, that "crowd" had been less than half a dozen.

"I'll bet. But really, I'm—"

"You ever find yourself feeling tired? Or a little under the weather, or just generally need a bit of a pick-me-up to get that job done?" Jesse rubbed at the bridge of his nose, sensing the sales pitch. "One sip of Tobias Henry Wilkerson's Miracle Boost will give you the energy of ten men! One sip and feel the burn of the secret elixirs as they give you the power, the speed, and the guile to get what you need done, DONE!"

"Great. You got any bullets for a Single Action Army?"

Tobias visibly shrank and his smile fell from his face as he realized his pitch had failed him. "Guess there's no fooling you."

"I've seen peddlers before. Don't take it personal. Out of interest, what's in the stuff?"

"Mostly just liquor and a huff of cocaine. You know, give you a boost and a bit of a buzz. But truth be told, this stuff isn't much good for anything but disinfecting wounds or starting fires. Keeps me from starving, though!" Tobias put the bottle back and returned to the rear of his wagon. He dug around, shuffling boxes of various sizes. "Rounds for a Colt SAA. What are they, a thirty-six?" Jesse nodded. "Now, I do have to confess: with the overwhelming popularity of the Single Action Army, it's often my first to sell out." Wilkerson stole a sideways glance at Jesse as he 'searched.' "You know, I have a Smith and Wesson in stock. I'd even throw in some ammunition, gratis, too."

"I've been polite enough. Now I'm gonna ask once more: do you have any of the rounds I'm after, or do I need to let Frank know that his generosity afforded to you has simply given you license to waste my time? I'm sure he'd be real pleased to hear that."

Tobias popped out from the back of the wagon. "Oh, would you look at that! A box of thirty-sixes!" He waved the box and the bullets inside rattled. "How foolish of me. They were right before my eyes! I beg an apology, sir. By no means was I attempting to humbug you." He shook the box again and then handed it to Jesse.

He opened it up and took out a cartridge. It didn't appear to have any signs of tampering or modification. The weight felt good, too. It was a common ruse to sell a box of bullets that contained anything but. One time they'd been nothing but spent casings. Another time, when Jesse was much younger, it was just a box of nails. "I'll take two boxes, please."

"Absolutely, Mr. Clayton," Wilkerson said as he accepted Jesse's money. "Now, what a day it has been! I feel it is time to hang up one's fiddle. Will I see you in the Jewel shortly?"

"Don't think you will," Jesse said, already walking away.

~

HE WAS JUST PASSING the Jewel when Frank Balfour stepped out onto his balcony, China cup in hand. Jesse pulled down on the brim of his Stetson, lowered his head and picked up his pace, but he knew it was in vain.

"Mr. Clayton, off so soon?" Franks' gravelly voice had a mischievous edge to it. Jesse looked up at him as Balfour took a sip, pinkie finger raised.

"Got my bullets," Jesse said, shaking the boxes. "Now's as good a time as any to get gone."

"Not without giving me a chance to win my money back! Get a table, I'll see you in five minutes! Then I'll lend you a horse to fetch yours from Squires."

As Frank disappeared, Jesse frowned. He didn't want to dally. Yet, the walk to Bill's farm was long, and the gray sky had turned a shade darker since he'd last paid it attention. Rain was coming. He could sacrifice a few dollars to save his legs an effort and himself a soaking.

What was the worst that could happen?

~

WHETHER IT WAS because of the weather or due to the day drawing to a close, the Jewel was starting to fill up. Jesse recognized none of the faces; most, if not all, of them must have been people on the road. They looked too tidy. Women in expensive dresses on the arms of men who looked down their noses at the place. They cast their judgment but still give Frank their money. There was no place else to go.

Jesse knocked back his drink and placed it on the bar next to his boxes of bullets. He put a finger up and signaled Big Dan to fill him up again. Frank was keeping him waiting, no doubt deliberately. The man was trying to unnerve him. Trying to get under his skin before they had even sat down. Balfour had already started playing, it seemed. Having underestimated Jesse before, this time he was going to play hard. Maybe even throw in the odd underhanded tactic. Already, he was testing Jesse's patience; would he be so averse to using his own establishment to gain an advantage?

Jesse regarded the table at which they would play. It was over on the far side of the Jewel, away from the piano and the main floor where people liked to dance and chat. But it was in clear view of the landing which lined two sides of the Jewel. He saw Wilkerson up there being led into a room by two of Frank's women.

Two of the seats at the poker table were easily viewed from up on that landing, while a third was exposed because of its proximity to the stairs. He'd make sure he sat with his back to the wall. Just to be on the safe side.

Of course, he could just cover his cards. But it was an easy thing to forget with plenty going on. Hell, Frank could even be fixing to rig the cards.

The question was: how much money was Jesse willing to lose?

He thought about all this as he loaded the bullets into his bandolier. He considered loading the Colt first, but given the current mood in town because of recent predicaments, Jesse decided against potentially scaring a room full of people. Especially when they had been drinking. Once he'd finished, he drank his refill and then turned to leave the bar.

That was when he saw Winona, and his mouth suddenly ran drier than a desert well in summer. Her hair was now tamed in long braids, and she was in a different dress. This one was blue, tight in the waist and blooming below—

Jesse was bumped by a passing patron. "Watch, it boy," the man slurred. It served to snap him out of his reverie, but now he saw that Winona had seen him from her position at the entrance. She walked his way, and he knew he had no chance of avoiding her now.

"Good evening, Winona. You look . . . great." Jesse was amazed he had managed that.

"You were gonna leave without seeing me again, weren't you?" Her words sounded as stern as her face, where her lips were pressed into a thin grimace. She looked him up and down and caught sight of his bandolier. "I see you got your bullets. Tell me this, Jesse. If your horse weren't currently tethered to my daddy's porch, would you still be here?"

"No." What else could he say? For some reason, he found himself unable to lie to her. Like he knew she'd see through it as easily as her bedroom window.

There was the slightest flicker in her frown. A brief softening in her eyes that revealed she was upset. It made his chest tighten in a way he didn't like.

"I'm sorry, Winona, I'm just—"

"Passing through. I know." Her tone had turned neutral. The tautness of her face relaxed as she glanced over at the piano. An old man was just settling down to it. "Hey. How about that dance?"

"Oh, I don't know . . . I'm about to play cards."

Winona grabbed him by the arm and said, "Nope, I ain't taking no excuses. I probably won't ever see you again, Jesse Clayton, and I ain't lettin' you slip through my fingers without so much as a dance."

He didn't fight it as she led him over to the middle of the saloon. The keys of the piano were janky and off key at first as the old man stretched his fingers, or whatever it was musicians did to warm up.

Then the melody came proper. Sweet and punchy. Winona took the lead as she held his hand and his waist, pulling him this way, that way, forward and back. She had grace in her every step while he stumbled through the motions, trying his best to keep up. She laughed and smiled through it, and sure enough, Jesse was smiling and laughing, too.

The song ended and Winona twirled away from him and bowed. This drew an applause from a few onlookers, and Jesse joined in as well. She came back to him, panting and smiling.

"You sure made the most of that, Winona," Jesse said as he caught his breath. "I think I was more a man-a-hanging."

"You did just fine. And thank you for my dance, Mr. Clayton. Now go on, somebody's waiting for you." She nodded toward the stairs and the poker table.

God damn it.

Frank was sitting on the chair with his back to the wall, there was a dealer seated on his left, and on his right sat Sullivan Crane. So much for the strategizing beforehand.

"Thank you for the dance, Winona. You've really set me up for the night."

∼

Jesse sat down at the table. Both men regarded him with grins while the feeble-looking dealer busied himself shuffling the deck.

"Nice of you to join us, Mr. Clayton." Frank said. "I was beginning to think you were having second thoughts. Lovely dancing, might I add."

"Yes," Sullivan added. "Quite the two left feet." Both men hooted at this.

Jesse wrestled back the need to respond. That would be exactly what the pair of them wanted. Get him riled and fixing to chide them instead of focusing on his cards. Best thing to do was to stay calm. Say nothing, and at least try his fair best to take a few more dollars from Frank. Relieving Crane of some wouldn't hurt, either. Having seen his house, finished or not, the man could certainly afford to lose some money.

"I'm glad you enjoyed it, gentleman. When's the last time either of you enjoyed the company of a woman you hadn't paid for?" Jesse said.

The two men's smiles disappeared.

"Five-dollar buy in," Frank said.

"That's more than I took from you yesterday," Jesse replied.

"This ain't a friendly game, son," Crane said, smoke curling around his words. He took another draw on his cigar. "You're playing for real this time. Now, pump up your money or run along and dance with your girlie. Don't be wasting our time."

Jesse dug a hand into the inside of his frock coat and pulled out some notes. He thumbed through them and tossed five dollars onto the table. The dealer took the money with a sweep of one hand and then deposited a stack of chips in front of Jesse with the other.

He picked up his stack and rolled them through his fingers. They were wooden, shoddily painted, and coarse enough to risk a splinter. They were very rough on the edges, too. Whoever had done the cutting had an interesting idea of a what 'round' was supposed to mean. Probably used gator teeth to do it, too. Still, this was just another pointless thing to rue. A needless thing to irk him. There was money to be made—or lost, mind you—at this table. These men at his front and left weren't easy marks, either. Jesse had a mind to think that there was no way Frank was letting anyone leave that table before somebody was empty handed. He wanted his money back and a bit more on top.

It was all amicable at first, everybody winning their fair share of hands. They were practically taking it in turns with the way the cards kept coming up. Jesse paid no mind to them; he watched his opponents. He saw the way Crane liked to chuckle when he got a favorable hand . . . and then bet big. Or how quiet he was when he meant to fold.

Frank, however, showed him nothing. Just stared right back at Jesse with those predatory eyes of his. He wasn't going to let anything slip.

It was the eighth hand where things took a turn for the tense. They'd drawn in quite a crowd; folks had peeled away from the piano or the bar to come and watch how this was all going to play out. Sullivan was hurting pretty bad; he'd been bleeding chips steadily all evening. He gave up on his cigar pretty quick; apparently, his mind could not quite stretch to smoking *and* poker. Jesse had lost a big hand but had made his way back, mostly thanks to Sullivan. Frank sat pretty with his big stack, his whiskey, and a big, satisfied grin on his face.

"I'm all in," Sullivan grumbled. He pushed his paltry pile of chips almost as far away from himself as he could. That was a man who wasn't confident of getting them back.

"Well, now, that's about the boldest you've been all night, Sullivan, it's nice to see you splurge on something that isn't somebody's property," Frank said through his grin. The mayor responded with a scowl as he fished for a fresh cigar.

"Call," Jesse said as he threw in his matching stake.

"You know, I am curious," Frank said. "Just what did the two of you talk about on your little visit to his big house? I'll bet it's real nice. He try to buy you, too, Jesse?" Frank laughed and then drank. He waved Big Dan over for a refill.

"How dare you!" Sullivan protested. His face had grown red. He looked like a plump tomato. He looked at Jesse, "Has this fine gentleman next to me supplied you with dope yet? Or one of his women?"

"Calm down, Sullivan, you look like you're liable to pop," Frank said. "There's nothing wrong with what I supply. For those so forlorn in their fortunes that they want to forget their troubles a while with what little they earn, I'm happy to provide that service. At least I'm not short-changing them for their homes."

Jesse looked on as the two men eyed each other.

"Dope? No," Jesse said coolly to finally break things off between the two of them. "A woman? Yes." Jesse ran his thumb and index finger across his jaw. "She did a great job of this."

"You're welcome, honey." It was Christie. She was leaning over his shoulder as she put down a fresh round of whiskey on the table. Her mousey hair fell across her face to hide that bruise, but Jesse had noticed the plunging neckline of her dress instead. He pulled his gaze away only to meet Frank's eyes again. He tilted his head in approval.

Christie placed a hand on Jesse's shoulder. He felt it as she gave it a little squeeze as she wished him good luck and winked at him. She certainly knew how to leave an impression.

"Hey, you keep staring I'll have to charge. It's your bet."

Frank's words pulled him back. He hadn't even realized he'd been watching her. As he looked back, he saw Winona. She looked away uncomfortably, busied herself with her drink. Hell, if that didn't make his guts ache.

She moved around the crowd to other side of the table and Frank, and as she dropped off his drink, she whispered something in his ear. Frank had his eyes on Jesse the whole time.

Oh, hell.

He hadn't been paying attention to anything but her. Had she been able to see his cards when she'd leaned in? God damn it, he had a great hand, too.

"I fold," Jesse said. A few in the crowd looked at each other quizzically.

"Well, Sullivan, seems like cowardice is catching tonight." Frank leaned over and started to scoop up his winnings.

"Nope. I just don't like being cheated."

This stopped Frank dead in his tracks. "Pardon me?" Frank spoke like the words had teeth of their own. The silence in the Jewel was audible now.

"That little trick with Christie, having her look at my cards?"

Frank raised his finger like a blade. "You listen here. If you think I'm gonna accept such accusations upon *my* character in *my* establishment, then you've got another think coming, *Clayton*." This was a fresh side to Frank. The wrinkles in his face had become ridges. His teeth were bared in a snarl, and he spat every word. And the use of his surname.

"Come on, don't play coy, Frank. If there ain't nothing foul afoot here, tell me what she said."

Frank's scowl burned across his face. As his eyes flitted around those gathered, he saw the concern drawn across theirs. Beneath the table, Jesse found his hand sliding toward his hip. As he did so, he spotted Big Dan reach for something below the bar.

Frank leaned back and blew out a sigh. "She was asking if she could shave something else of yours tonight." He let the sentence sit for a beat. Then he snapped his head back and roared laughter. The crowd erupted, too. Among shoulder slaps and whoops, Jesse could feel the tension lift away from the room. It felt easier to breathe. He even let slip a smirk himself. With a sentence, Frank had turned a room on its head.

"You've got a point, my friend," Frank said as the laughter died down. "In the spirit of good nature, and being the good-natured and fair-spirited man I am, I offer up a chance to win it back. Not just what you've lost, but all of it. One game: winner takes all." Frank held out his hands to the room. "How does that sound, everybody?"

The crowd whooped and hollered. Jesse spied Winona close to the back, struggling to see.

"Well, how 'bout it, Mr. Clayton? I had you about cleaned out. What say you rise from the ashes, see if you can't give these people a show?"

Jesse nodded. The crowd cheered.

"Now, if I just settle up with you first, Sullivan. What have you got?" Frank said.

"Two pair: kings and eights," Sullivan said as he flipped his cards.

"Bad luck," Frank said. "I've got trip' Eights."

Sullivan sighed and got up from his chair. His belly nudged the table as he maneuvered out of the space and trotted toward the bar.

Jesse would have had the son of a gun. Jesse hadn't felt a sting like that since his days as a kid. He'd been cheated in card games he'd play with his brother, who'd relieve him of what few pennies he'd scoured the dirty floors of saloons for.

"So how does this go, Frank?" Jesse asked.

Frank stood and straightened his jacket. He gestured to the dealer for the deck. "You take this, and you shuffle as good as you can." Frank pushed the deck across the faded felt. Jesse picked it up and did as he was bid. "You pick a card. I pick a card. Whoever's is highest, wins."

"Really? That's how we're gonna do it?"

"Only way I can think you won't cry that I'm cheatin' you."

Jesse placed the deck on the table and with both hands spread the cards around until he'd good and covered most of it. He looked up at Frank, who nodded. They both reached for a card.

Jesse picked his and looked. The face of the king of hearts was smiling up at him, one corner all dog-eared. He put it down on the table and people in the crowd gasped. One drunken onlooker cheered.

Frank raised an eyebrow.

"Would you look at that," Frank said as he considered his own card and Jesse's king. Jesse didn't much like that pondering look on the man's face. "I feel it's important to resolve something before I put my card down."

Jesse folded his arms and frowned. "What, exactly?"

"Are aces high or low?" Frank said, and his grin returned. "Remind me again?"

Well, he certainly wasn't cheating this time. But god damn his luck that a fifty-fifty shot for everything or nothing would see his king lose out to an ace. Jesse gritted his teeth as his gaze wandered the crowd and he settled on Winona, who looked as hopeless as he felt.

"High."

"Right you are," Frank said as he turned his card around. "Not that it matters. Looks like neither of us is going home empty handed." He tossed his card onto the table.

The king of spades.

There was another cheer, and Jesse couldn't help but laugh. "You had me there. Damn it, you had me, Frank." He reached out a hand and Frank firmly shook it.

"Christie, take these chips upstairs and take care of Mr. Clayton's money, please," Frank instructed, then he said to Jesse, "Now, let's go have another drink!" Frank clapped an arm around his shoulder and escorted Jesse from the table. As they approached the bar, there were shoulder slaps and handshakes a plenty.

Just as Jesse neared Winona he heard a loud wail and a crash. Jesse looked toward the front of the saloon to see Sullivan on the floor and a table overturned next to him. Standing over him was probably the largest man Jesse had ever seen.

7
―――

THE SLIGHTEST OF KNOTS

'Slim Joe' was an ironic name. The man who stood at the entrance of the Jewel, towering over the cowering lump that was Sullivan Crane, was anything but slim. Easily six-feet-five-inches, the man was taller and wider than Big Dan, who was the size of a grizzly. Cullen wore a felt derby hat which had to have been custom made given the size of the man's head. It was scuffed and dirty, much like the tan on his face that wasn't hidden underneath his bushy sideburns. His coat and trousers hugged him tight; they were patched up and frayed around the joints. Jesse didn't want to imagine the smell. Slim Joe grinned as he looked around the place, revealing teeth that varied in shades of brown and yellow. One front tooth was chipped, giving it a dagger-like edge. In that gap rested a toothpick.

Joe stepped forward, his boots thumping the floorboards, and in followed his friends, six in all. Among them were the two Jesse had run into before, the Foy twins, Dustin and George.

"Evenin', Mayor. Always a pleasure," Joe said and plucked the toothpick out of his mouth. He hawked a brown glob at the floor just past Crane's head before popping the toothpick back in his mouth. He turned away from the mayor and raised his voice to address the whole saloon. "Listen up, everybody. Let's not make any rash decisions or try to do anything untoward." He eyeballed people as he scanned the crowd, then took a man's drink and knocked it back. "We wouldn't want nobody ending up like your sheriff, now would we?"

Joe clicked his fingers, and his gang drew their guns and pulled out sacks. They started to make their way through the people. They brandished their irons, pressed barrels into faces and threatened harm to anyone uncooperative. The patrons of the Jewel began to offer up their dollars and their valuables.

Jesse waited as Joe made his way toward him, passing people with threatening glares and guttural laughs. Jesse glanced at Frank, who was watching Joe with a frown, then at Winona, who was looking at *him*. She had a pleading look in her eyes. He felt the slightest of knots tighten in his belly. He chose to ignore it.

He winked at her as he slowly wrapped his hand around the grip of his Colt. He plucked it gently from its holster, and its weight felt almost reassuring. It was then that Jesse remembered he had yet to load it.

Oh, hell.

There was no time now as Slim Joe was almost in front of him, just a few steps away, his huge frame blocking out almost everything else. He knew this town's trouble was none of his business and that personally he had no quarrel with this Cullen. He was supposed to be just passing through. But he had just won a lot of money that would see him living comfortable a while. Jesse wasn't about to give that up to nobody.

Here goes nothing.

Jesse stepped out and faced Slim Joe, careful to have his free hand clasped over the barrel of his gun. There was no need to advertise the fact that the chambers of it were indeed empty. Once again, he was going to try and bluff his way out of trouble. The thought occurred to him that his luck was long overdue to run out with this gambit.

"Nobody's giving up anything today, Mr. Cullen." Jesse stated. "So why don't you and your men here just walk on out and enjoy the rest of your evening."

Joe stopped in his tracks. His mouth hung agape for a moment, the toothpick hanging off his bottom lip. Jesse could see the other end of it, all chewed up and broken.

The man was so slow Jesse could almost read his mind. First, he would spit another delightful wad of brown, then he would reach for his iron with the means to shoot Jesse dead. Slim Joe did the former, after dragging up a truly awful noise from the back of his throat.

Jesse saw him start to reach down and pointed his Colt. "I wouldn't."

Cullen eyed him with bulbous, bloodshot eyes. He straightened himself slowly and then folded his arms, further straining the poor fibers of his jacket. "And why's that, partner?"

"You reach for that it'll be the last thing you do. I guarantee it."

"Hey, Boss," came a familiar voice from behind Cullen. Must have been one of the Foy twins was Jesse's guess. "We know that guy. That's the feller what stopped us the other night."

"Really now?" Cullen said. A disgusting smile of yellow and brown bloomed across his face as he titled his head with intrigue. "You're the one who done threatened my boys? Got 'em all scared as to the fact you weren't afeared o' bein' outnumbered?" Cullen laughed. "Well, I wonder if you got that kinda balls when it's seven to one instead of two, boy."

"You mean six," Jesse stated. Again, he kept his tone flat. He couldn't show this man a glimpse of anything. He tightened his grip around the Colt to stave off the shakes.

The toothpick rolled from one corner of Cullen's chapped lips to the other. "How do you mean there ... *boy*?"

Jesse smiled. With the way Cullen said boy he knew he had the man-giant's attention now. "You don't count." Jesse shrugged as he said it. "Seeing as you'll be the first I put a bullet in. You'll be dead before you even get a finger to your gun, Mr. Cullen."

Cullen's face twisted into something even less welcoming. "Really now? I think my boys here would deliver a mighty retribution to you in the case o' you allotting to bed me down." He spat at the floor to punctuate his point.

Jesse nodded slowly. "They would. But not without me taking at least two, maybe even three of them down before I do. But I do believe, Mr. Cullen, on account of your being a little soft there in the head . . ." Jesse tapped his forehead twice real slow, to really put it across. ". . . if you or your men do anything other than turn on your heels and leave this establishment, and in turn, the fine town of Fortune, you'll leave me no choice but to put a bullet in you. And I don't often miss."

Cullen chuckled and scratched at his wild sideburn. His men were on edge, gripping their pistols as if to strangle them, shifting from foot to foot, darting their eyes between each other, their boss, Jesse, and anyone else that dared do more than blink.

"Say that I didn't believe you, boy . . . that I thought that this peppy little dog here wouldn't hunt. Not one bit. What would you say to that?"

Jesse answered by thumbing back the hammer on his Colt. Cullen stiffened and swallowed. His eyes narrowed, and his big nostrils flared.

For a moment, nobody moved. The whole saloon stood still and silent.

"What's your name, boy?"

"Jesse Clayton."

"You got a real nice hat and coat there, Jesse Clayton," Cullen said. He lapped his tongue over his chipped tooth. "Be a shame to spoil it when I leave you dyin' in the mud. Ain't gone be right now, mind you. No use turnin' this place into a bucket o' blood. But you keep an eye out now, boy. We gone see each other again, you can guarantee that. And I'm gonna enjoy it when we do. Not so sure you will." Cullen flashed another disgusting grin.

He turned and started to walk toward the entrance. His men lowered their weapons and started to file out of the Jewel before him. He passed the still-prone Crane and moved to deal him a swift kick. When Crane whimpered and flinched, Cullen held back his foot and chuckled, shaking his head. Just as he reached the threshold, he turned back.

"You people of Fortune," he said with a sweeping gesture of his hands to them all before pointing a thick and dirty finger at Jesse. "You have this man here to thank today as you get to keep your wares and your dollars. But know we will come back to collect . . . with interest. Goodbye now!" Cullen tipped his hat and disappeared into the evening.

Again, it was silent in the Jewel. Nobody spoke or even dared to move as they listened to the footsteps outside in the mud, the grunts and voices, and then finally the rapid-fire sloppy claps of hooves on mud as the gang rode away.

For a moment, Jesse felt the eyes of the entire saloon upon him.

Frank stepped up beside him and began clapping. Winona joined in, and so did the whores. Soon enough, the crowd joined in, too, and Jesse was the recipient of a raucous ovation. Even Crane managed to clap from the floor. Frank put an arm on his shoulder and pulled him in close.

"I'm not sure whether you've got balls made of brass, you're off your nut . . . or both!" Frank said. He patted Jesse's chest and laughed. "Now, are you sure I can't get you a girl after that little show you put on?" Ellie is really good with her hands, you know."

"That sounds real nice, Frank," Jesse said. "But again, I'm afraid I'm gonna have to decline. If you'll excuse me, I'm gonna head outside and catch some air, and maybe make sure there ain't nobody tarrying around out there looking to put another hole in me."

Clayton stepped away from Frank and politely moved through the crowd that had clustered around him following his victorious exchange with the outlaw Cullen. He accepted handshakes, pats on the back and various utterances of 'congratulations,' 'well done' and 'goddamn, you're brave,' as he pushed through them to get outside.

The cool air out there was icy crisp as it hit his lungs. He almost stumbled down the steps into the mud of the street as he realized he was overcome with giddiness.

He doubled over as he felt his heart running with all the might of a steam engine. It didn't feel like it meant to stop. He took deep, gulping breaths to calm himself down but it wasn't abating the sickly rising in his stomach. Something was coming up, and he wasn't sure he had much say in the matter.

That was when he felt a hand on his back.

"You okay, Jesse?" Winona's sweet voice cut right through the noise of the pounding drums of his heartbeat. She eased him back up and looked him dead in the eye. "Now you look at me. You breathe in through your nose and then out through your mouth."

He did as he was bid. In through the nose, slowly. Then out the mouth just as steady.

"Come on now, this ain't no different than havin' one too many whiskeys. Just breathe, Jesse." She kept saying it and he focused on the words. He felt the that sickly rising slide from the top his chest back down into his stomach. The drums in his ears began to fade away, too.

Jesse let out one long, last exhale and then righted himself. "Thank you, Winona."

"You know, if I didn't know any better, I'd say you were feelin' scared." Winona's warm hand still had a hold of his, not that he was going to mention it.

"You're damn right I was," Jesse said and showed her his Colt.

She saw the empty chambers and her eyes widened. "Jesus Christ, Jesse, are you *crazy*? No wonder you're actin' worse than a cat in a room full of rockers. I thought you'd got some bullets from Wilkerson?"

"I did, just didn't feel the need to load up my Colt right away."

"Why?"

"I had to go play cards. Speakin' of which, I need to get my winnings from Frank."

"No." Winona's voice had a sternness to it Jesse had only heard when she was addressing her father. "That can wait. You load up that Colt and then you take me to get some dinner. I'm starving and don't feel like eating alone."

At the very mention of food Jesse's stomach warbled and growled. Apparently, he was outnumbered two to one.

"Well, all right then, Winona," Jesse conceded.

He opened the loading gate on his Colt and pulled the hammer to half-cock, which freed up the cylinder to move. He plucked bullets from his bandolier and loaded them, keeping one chamber empty to prevent any accidents. He snapped the loading gate back and holstered the Colt in one swift movement.

"Well, ain't you a steady hand. What else are they that assured with?" Winona asked.

"Well . . ." Jesse faltered. He cleared his throat and adjusted his Stetson, which was already straight enough. He was trying to fetch up an answer as he felt the cool splashes of rain dropping on him. He looked up as the drops began to increase in number. "Looks like we'd better move this on to inside." The drops turned swiftly into a torrent, and Jesse saw only one option. He took off his hat, put it on Winona's head, and removed his coat. "Put this on!" he said over the rush of the rain as he draped it coat over her shoulders.

"There's no need. The hotel's but a small ways down the road," Winona protested.

"Yeah, but it's plenty easier for me to dry than it is for you, Winona."

Jesse had his arm around her waist as he helped her navigate the mud that was swiftly dissolving into a sloppy mess under the hammering rain. With every step, they flicked up water and mud as they crossed the street. Winona slipped just before they reached the hotel, and her leg went from under her. Jesse reached for the beam of the veranda with his free hand as he pulled her to him. Having prevented a muddy catastrophe, he helped her straighten up and then they stepped under cover of the hotel's balcony.

"Jesse, you're soaked!" Winona said, laughing.

"Well, that tends to happen when it's raining this hard," Jesse replied. He ran his fingers through his hair, sweeping back the long dark tendrils behind his ears.

"Yeah, it's a real gully washer," Winona agreed.

He watched droplets of rain run down her cheeks like tears. He wondered how strange it was to see that alongside her pretty smile. He could hear a distant thumping and supposed it was the drumming of his heart again. He didn't mind. She moved to take off his frock coat, but he stopped her, telling her it would help keep the heat in until they got inside. That was ballyhoo, but she didn't need to know that; he liked the way she looked in it.

They watched a thoroughly soaked Wilkerson hold his hat as he ran from his wagon up to the hotel, throwing splashes of sloppy muck in his wake. He collected himself as he found cover, then bid Jesse and Winona a good evening and entered the hotel.

Once Wilkerson was inside, Jesse looked back at her. She seemed to be working up the courage to say something. The thumping grew louder, yet he did not feel the drums in his chest. Must have been the cold—it was creeping into his bones.

"Would you come with me?" Winona said at last. "If I were to leave here, and do like what we talked about last night?"

"You're persistent, Winona, I'll give you that." He knew from the look in her eyes that he wasn't going to talk his way around the subject.

The truth was, he wasn't sure what to say. He thought she was pretty. He liked being around her. He'd never really talked to a girl in this way as much as he had Winona. He'd been in the company of wayward female outlaws while bringing them in on a bounty, and of other hunters he'd worked with in the past. He'd not really had friends, more like acquaintances. But in spite of only knowing her for a day and change, Winona didn't feel like *just* a friend.

Problem was, he couldn't tell her that. He could try, but his throat was threatening to run dry again and his lips slammed shut the moment he'd go to talk, even in all this rain. But if he could speak, what the hell would he say, when he couldn't even figure out his feelings?

That thumping was louder than ever. Jesse put a hand to his heart and felt the quick beat, but not *that* quick. The hell was making that noise then?

"You okay, Jesse?" Winona asked. She stepped closer to him and swept a rogue strand of his hair behind his ear.

Jesse's eyes shifted beyond Winona's left shoulder as a rider on horseback emerged, having been blocked from view by Wilkerson's parked wagon. He realized then—all too late—what the thumping was.

The figure drew from the hip as their horse splashed up mud and water.

"Nice coat there, boy!" the figure yelled as it raised a pistol.

There wasn't time. He lunged at Winona as the rider's pistol boomed. She yelped as Jesse wrapped around her and pulled her down with him. They both hit the decking with a wet slap. The rider laughed as his horse tore off down the street.

Jesse pulled himself away from Winona as she lay next to him. As he did so, he felt a rushing warmth from her and saw that he was wet again.

Wet with blood.

8

A SHOWER OF ALCOHOL AND GLASS

"Winona . . . Winona!" Jesse said as he kneeled over her. "Winona, can you hear me?" He checked her over but with his coat and the thickness of her dress, it was hard to tell where the blood was coming from. He felt his heart race anew as he tried rousing her.

The hotel door opened and out came Dalby and Wilkerson with two other men.

"What's happened?" Wilkerson asked.

"She's been shot. Help me get her inside."

The five of them lifted her as carefully as they could and took her through reception and into the back room, which Dalby said was his. They were putting her down onto the bed when they heard the report of a gunshot outside, then the cracking of two more. The men all glanced toward the front of the hotel, then back to each other.

"Any of you a doctor?" Jesse demanded.

"I was a medic in the war. You might be best off helping with whatever's outside," Wilkerson said while looking at the Colt in Jesse's hand.

He didn't remember drawing it. "But what about her?"

"I'll do what I can, but I won't be all too effective if whatever is out there winds up in here!" Wilkerson rattled. "And will somebody get me some water, towels and something to cut with that's clean? And—"

Jesse didn't catch the rest as he raced out of the room and back into the street. Sitting there worrying about her wouldn't do any good. But he could do something out here, maybe even catch that bastard Cullen who did this. He had an aim. That kept him focused.

When Jesse was focused, he was deadly.

Back out in the street, he caught the tail end of an exchange at the Jewel. Big Dan and a few others were behind cover, firing at retreating riders.

Jesse was about to move when he heard the rapid wet pounding of mud from another horse. It emerged from behind Wilkerson's wagon, and the rider had his pistol aimed at Jesse. He backed into the cover of the doorway as the man let loose his barrage. Splinters of wood showered him as the rounds punched into the frame and smashed through panes of glass.

Jesse stepped out and took aim at the man, thumbed back the hammer of his Single Action Army and settled his aim as the rider pulled away. He squeezed the trigger and the man slumped forward on his horse before falling off. The horse kept going, though, dragging the limp body through the mud as it cantered out of town.

Across the way, the other two riders were long gone. Big Dan and the others looked to be reloading their guns.

This wasn't over yet, it seemed.

Jesse heard more sets of thumping hooves coming, then he spied the two riders from the Jewel circling back. He ran over to the Wilkerson wagon for cover against the oncoming riders. As he got there, he found that the doors on the front had been forcibly opened. A few bottles of tonic lay in the mud.

Up ahead at the Jewel, they began exchanging fire again as the riders galloped toward them. Jesse waited as the horses came tearing past the wagon. He thumbed the hammer and fired, and then fired again. His bullets went wide of their marks. The rain was throwing off his aim. He rounded the wagon as the riders turned and fired back. More splinters flew, and he made a mental note to apologize to Wilkerson once this was all done.

If you don't end up fulla bullets, that is.

Jesse leaned out from the cover of the wagon and fired two more shots. Both found their mark as one rider threw his arms up and screamed. His shotgun fell into the mud alongside him.

The other riders reached the Jewel, and that was when Jesse saw one of them heft something alight. It was a flaming bottle. He looked down at the bottles around his feet and then up again as the rider threw the bottle upwards. It pinwheeled in the air and crashed through one of the upper windows of the Jewel. There was a second crash and a roaring *whoosh!* Suddenly, that room bloomed with a fierce yellow blaze. Jesse heard screams as he saw flames lick at the windowsills, growing bigger with each passing second.

Something moved inside. A flaming shape burst through the broken window and onto the balcony. The howls of pain made it clear that it was a man, as he scrambled, patting himself frantically, toward the railing. Rain sizzled as it pelted his flaming skin as he broke through the balustrade and plummeted head-first into the mud. He splashed into it, and his body twitched and spasmed as it continued to burn. Then he lay still as the mud sizzled and bubbled around him. The riders laughed and tore off down as a handful of men rushed out to kick mud over the burned man. The flames crackled and spluttered, before finally hissing away to nothing.

The riders were turning in the distance, all of them, six by Jesse's count, gathering for a ride in. They formed a line and began to ride in for another pass.

"Get back inside! They're coming back!" Jesse shouted to the men. "Quickly, now!" When he saw them file back inside, Jesse quickly took in his surroundings. Plenty of balconies and rooftops to serve him well. He was gonna put up a fight before they left.

Jesse bent and pulled a bottle of Wilkerson's miracle tonic from out of the mud, then he ran back into the hotel. He crossed the foyer and headed up the stairs, rounded the landing and shouldered the door open out onto the balcony. There, he dropped to his haunches and waited. He had about thirty seconds before they got to him, by his estimation. He used the time to reload and to get a hold of his breath. He took long and slow ones to help steady his racing heart, timing it with the thumbing of rounds into the chambers of his Colt. He focused on the chills from the rainwater running down his spine.

The sound of splashing hooves was upon him. He popped out from his hiding place and saw the six riders, all clumped together in a tight V-formation.

Just like he'd hoped.

They'd spotted him now, and as they raised their guns to shoot him down, he did not match their efforts. Instead, with his left hand he grabbed the tonic bottle by its long neck and took aim for the rider in the middle. He tossed it in a long looping arc, and then as the bottle cartwheeled through the air to meet the rider, he drew his Colt with his right hand. He took aim as he thumbed back the hammer. Then he squeezed the trigger.

The bottle shattered into a shower of alcohol and glass fragments. The man in the middle took the brunt of it. He clutched his face and screamed as he rolled backwards off his horse and into the mud. The two riders either side of him took a few shards of glass as they covered their faces instead of firing up at Jesse. The other three were unfazed by Jesse's gambit. They fired at him, and he pulled back and hugged the floor.

As soon as they stopped, he was up. He sprinted across the balcony and vaulted it onto the neighboring building as he gave chase to the other riders. They began to pull away as he vaulted the rail onto the next building. He kept running as his lungs started to burn and his legs protested his efforts. Another railing vaulted and the riders were still pulling away. Jesse knew he'd get no closer, so he halted and brought up his Colt, supporting his wrist with his left hand as he took aim on the riders. His Colt barked twice, and his bullets found nothing but mud. His breathing was too unsteady and was sending his aim awry.

The riders tore away into the falling rain and the fading light of dusk. There was no use wasting any more bullets on a wayward shot, and by the time he'd be steady enough to make it count, they'd have been long gone anyway.

Jesse turned back to look at the town. There was still a glow from that upstairs window at the Jewel. He dropped from the balcony and ran down Main Street. On his way to the Jewel, he came upon the rider who had taken the face full of glass. He was still writhing around in the mud, moaning, and clutching his face. Blood coated his hands and fingers.

"You okay there, friend?" Jesse said, not all too friend-like.

The man responded with a wail of pain as he continued to thrash his legs in the mud. Eventually, he said, "Please, help me please. There's glass in my face!"

Jesse was about to respond when he caught sight of Big Dan and Frank approaching. Dan was covered in soot that was running off in the rain, while Frank was shirtless, a shotgun slung across his back.

"This one of them?" Frank said. Jesse could see, now he was closer, that Frank was bleeding from a cut across his head. The man paid it no mind, but his eyes burned with a hell-fury Jesse hadn't seen in him before. "One of them riders?"

Jesse nodded.

"What's his problem?"

"There's glass in his face," Jesse answered. "On account of me."

"Right." Frank shot Jesse a nod of appreciation. "We can help with that back at the saloon. Get you all patched up . . . friend. Got a few things I'd like to talk about, while we're at it." Frank's voice had taken on an unsettling, forced pleasantness. He looked at Jesse and said, "You don't mind me relieving you of this burden, do you?"

"Not at all."

"Good," Frank said flatly. He turned away. "Dan. Bring him."

Without a word, Big Dan bent over and, with one dinner-plate-sized hand, grabbed the injured rider by the calf. He then began to follow Frank, dragging the man behind him.

"You okay, Frank?" Jesse called after him over the man's moaning.

"Christie was in that room they burned."

Jesse's breath caught. He rubbed at his chin as he watched Frank and Big Dan walk on, dragging the wounded man behind them.

9

THE SHELTER FROM SIN

Christie was dead. Just hours ago, she was serving drinks. A day ago, she'd held a blade to his neck. She had been laughing, smiling. *Living*. And now she was gone. Jesse couldn't help but blame himself. If he'd shot the rider with the bottle, things might have turned out a fair ways different. The thought made his stomach twist.

As the last ebbs of adrenaline left him, a wave of tiredness crashed over him. His legs felt full of sand, and now he felt the cold again, and he shivered. The heavens continued to fall as he stood there, teeth chattering, his mind wandering. His thoughts ambled their way to Winona.

God, Winona!

He raced back along Main Street and burst into the hotel. He tracked mud in his wake as he ran into the back room. Wilkerson spun around on his chair and delivered about the fiercest shushing Jesse had ever received. Flecks of spittle flew from his mouth either side of a bony finger he had pressed to his lips.

Jesse raised his hands in apology.

"Keep it down, please," Wilkerson said, his voice hushed. "She's sleeping, and that is the very best thing she can do right now to aid her recovery."

"You mean—" Something caught in Jesse throat. "You mean, she's okay? She's not dead . . . or dying?"

"No, Mr. Clayton, sir. I believe she has been rather fortunate. A feat which appears to be something of a rarity in this town, in my experience at least." He stood from his chair and retrieved his hat from the back of it. "From what I gather, the shooter didn't have the best of aim, much to Ms. Squires's benefit, as what could have been a fateful shot to the heart was instead a rather nasty glancing shot across her chest. She has you to thank for that, I suppose?"

Jesse nodded.

"How fortunate she is to have a guardian such as you. I've cleaned the wound and dressed it. She'll have a terrible scar and a hell of a story to tell. But long as it's kept clean, that will be as bad as it gets."

Jesse blew out a long sigh.

"I trust the . . . *activities* outside have reached a satisfying conclusion?"

Jesse nodded. "But you might want to poke around the Jewel. Might be some folks that need a hand like yours before the night's through."

The salesman nodded and then put on his hat. "That I will. If I do not see you, goodnight, Mr. Clayton, and might I suggest something?"

"Sure."

"Get some sleep yourself. You look dreadfully tired."

A scoff escaped Jesse's lips. "Can't fight you on that one."

"And yet, I imagine you'll probably spend most of this night watching her every breath, lest she inhale the wrong way."

"I'm just here to make sure she's all right, is all."

"Yes, of course, you are, Mr. Clayton. I could tell that from how you burst your way in here. I'll see myself out." Wilkerson left the room and closed the door gently behind him, a marked contrast to the manner of Jesse's entrance.

Alone with Winona, for a moment he watched her lying on her side, her eyes closed. She looked so peaceful. A bed sheet had been pulled over her to spare her decorum, for part of her garment had been cut away and was strewn across the floor, along with his hat and his frock coat. Jesse pulled the chair a little closer to the bed and sat on it.

He watched the little strand of hair hanging across her face gently rise and fall with each steady breath. He saw her pinky finger twitch slightly. He gingerly reached out and saw his hand was still dripping wet. He wiped it off on the bed sheet and then he gently clasped her hand.

She felt so warm.

"I'm sorry, Winona," Jesse said, just above a whisper. "This is my fault you're like this. I didn't mean for it, and I hope you'll forgive me. You're not the only one who got hurt tonight on account o' me, neither. A man and Christie was burned alive, and that's on me twice over. I shot the wrong man and If I hadn't . . . he wouldn't have thrown that bottle, and they would probably still both be alive here.

"And damn it, if I hadn't given you my coat then Cullen wouldn't have been shooting at you, either. But hell, I could have stopped all of this from ever even happening at all if I hadn't run my mouth in the Jewel. Frank wasn't doin' nothing. Nobody else was stepping up to do anything and I think . . . *why?* Why don't these people stand up for themselves when they outnumber these men? I realize now that's 'cause you have before and paid a toll. Just like the town has tonight because of my actions. I poked that ugly son of a gun, and he poked back a lot harder, didn't he?

"Well, I'll tell you this, Winona. He's not gonna get away with it. Slim Joe Cullen does not get away with hurting you and killin' Christie. And it's on me to settle that debt. I know I said I was just passing through, and it was the truth for a time. But these past few days, spending time here and . . . and with *you*, I realize I ain't passing through, I've just been running away.

"I ain't always been a good man, Winona. But for years, I've been trying to distance myself from all that, and do a little good here and there to put it right. Keep getting myself in scrapes like I did with you and your daddy, and I keep thinkin', one of these days it's gonna be the death of me."

Jesse shifted into more of a slouch, resting his chin on his shoulder. "Well, maybe it's time. And if it is, at least I'll go down trying to make things right."

He kept his eyes on her, but his eyelids felt awful heavy. Each blink seemed to stretch for longer and longer, until eventually Jesse slipped off to sleep.

A few moments later, Winona's hand squeezed back.

JESSE WOKE WITH A START. His flinching almost caused him to fall off the chair. The back room was dark, but light was creeping in through the open doorway. Fortunately for Jesse, Winona was still sleeping softly despite his eventful waking.

He stretched against the soreness in his neck and back and then quietly made his way into the hotel foyer. He saw no signs of Dalby or any patrons. He peeked into the dining room and saw it was empty as well.

Outside, the street was also eerily quiet. Thankfully, the rain had let up, and the sky had cleared for the most part, with only one menacing gray cloud among the sparse scattering above Fortune. Wilkerson's wagon looked just as it did the night before, bottles strewn in the mud and the door still hanging open. There wasn't a sign of anybody in the street, even outside the Jewel. Jesse could see the black scorching all around the room and part of the balcony where it had burned. The burning man had been removed from the street, hopefully to a more dignified place before he was finally laid to rest.

Jesse picked up the tonic bottles and put them back in the wagon before closing it up as best he could. It wasn't easy as the door had been forced open. When he was done, he walked down to the Jewel to see if he could find anybody.

The doors were in a sorry state, their window panes all but shot through, just a few shards still clinging to the edges, while the wood had whole chunks shot out of it. They had taken a heavy beating. The windows and the walls hadn't fared much better.

He pushed on through the doors and saw Big Dan standing

behind a bullet-riddled bar, picking up pieces of glass from a rack of broken bottles. At a table nearby sat Wilkerson as he tended to the grazes of one of Balfour's women. She was young and frail, and heavy dark bags hung underneath her eyes. She was covered in scratches, probably from scrambling away from the commotion. Her red hair was a mess all around her head, and her eyes looked glazed and vacant. Wilkerson looked to Jesse and offered a curt nod before returning to his work.

Jesse approached the bar, aware of the glass crunching like eggshells under his every step. He asked Big Dan where Frank was, and when the big man turned around, he said nothing, just nodded in the direction of a door upstairs.

His office, most likely.

"He's still having a . . . *conversation* with a man in there," Wilkerson said. Jesse felt his discomfort in the way he said conversation.

Jesse turned to him. "That man didn't happen to be bleeding some? From his face?"

"Certainly looked that way. He was halfway up the stairs by the time I got here. It got rather loud rather quick. It went quiet for a few hours but then it all kicked up again once the sun was up. I'd know. I've been up all night, cleaning and stitching."

A piercing howl emanated from Frank's office. That was the kind of sound that couldn't have come from just any man, Jesse thought. That feller was in a whole world of pain. Another howl made him wince.

"All night?"

"Yes, indeed. Didn't quite sound that bad at first, mind you . . ." Wilkerson paused as another shriek faded into a moan. "I believe Mr. Balfour may be running out of patience with the man."

Jesse pushed away from the bar and headed for the stairs. Big Dan moved with a speed Jesse hadn't known he was capable of as he maneuvered, with plenty of grace for a big man, to cut him off. He stood at the bottom of the stairs and folded his arms, then simply gave Jesse precisely one shake of his big head. Jesse noticed he still bore a few smudges of black from the previous night. With no sleep, Jesse thought it best not to test the big man this morning.

"Maybe I'll just sit back down . . . have a drink," he said has he retreated from Big Dan.

"Wise choice. I've already seen the results of what he can do to a man with his bare hands. I wouldn't go out back if I were you." Wilkerson yawned. "*Especially* if you've eaten this morning."

As Wilkerson talked, Jesse looked at Big Dan, who was still watching him from the bottom of the stairs. Big Dan smirked. Jesse wasn't going to try his luck against Dan, who may or may not have torn a man apart with his bare hands, judging by Wilkerson's implications. He thought about Cullen, and how he was even bigger, and made a mental note to keep the man at range when the time came. Jesse wasn't much for a fist fight against any man. Best not to get caught up in the wrath of Cullen's grasps if he could help it.

"I'll keep that in mind, thank you," Jesse said.

There was a noise upstairs again. The three men turned their attention to Frank's office as they tried to make sense of it. Like the howls before it, the door muffled much of the sound. It was a long, drawn-out whimper. The whimper became a whine. Another one. And then another and another, getting quicker and louder with each repetition. If Jesse didn't know any better, he would put that sound down to a man pleading for his life. The moaning culminated in one long cry which—

BLAM!

There was a soft thud. Then footsteps. Then the door to the office opened and out stepped Frank. He approached the balustrade and Jesse saw he had his sleeves rolled up. His hands were bloody. So was his face. Frank's eyes searched the saloon briefly until they settled on him.

"Ah, good," Frank said. Again, with a pleasantness that made feel uneasy. "Jesse, would you mind stepping into my office?" Jesse looked over at Big Dan. The man stepped away from the steps and back toward the bar. Jesse looked back up at Frank. "I think we have something rather important to discuss."

STEPPING into Frank's office for the first time, all Jesse could see was red. His attention was drawn to the man sitting in the chair in the middle of the room. His head was thrown back and his legs sagged as if he were asleep. He was bound to the chair, both he and the rope covered in his own blood, a lot more of which pooled around him, seeping into the floorboards.

"Quite the conversation you two had," Jesse said, still looking at the corpse in the chair.

"It was a riveting talk, indeed." Frank rounded his desk, a simple and rudimentary box when compared to the custom-made one Jesse had seen at Sullivan Crane's estate. He reached for a bottle sitting on it and took a long pull from it. He placed it down and coughed, wiped his mouth, and then sat down.

"If you were just talking, did you need to kill him?" Jesse asked.

Frank was rolling down his sleeves when he paused to look at Jesse with indignation. "Oh, I'm *sorry*, was I supposed to let this piece of low-life *scum* live?" He went back to his sleeves and continued in a softer tone. "That man was dead the moment you knocked him off his horse. You simply left the burden of finishing it to me. You're welcome for the shelter from sin, Jesse."

"I killed two other men," Jesse said.

Frank rose from his desk. "And they *killed Christie!*" He slammed a fist down. "They killed *my* sweet Christie. They took her away from *me*. And each one of those filthy saddle-bums is gonna pay for it, you have my word." Frank snatched up the bottle and took another pull. "I gave that bastard Cullen and his friends too much slack."

"You set them up to this?" Jesse asked.

Frank swallowed. The look of indignation had returned. "Are you stupid? Or are you just trying your best to look that way, Jesse?"

Jesse leaned back against the wall just beside the door. "Well, you do run dope. Seems that the Jewel is a great place for the gang to hit on the frequent when there's plenty of patrons to rob. Then said wronged folks drown their sorrows with more booze from your bar, if they have anything left, that is. Then you take a cut from the theft. Must about keep you afloat in a dying town alongside your dope running."

"*You* are off your *God-damned nut!*" Frank shook his head and laughed. "Have you been drinking Wilkerson's tonic? I can't think of any other way you'd be making so little sense. You're not from around here, Jesse, so I'll give you the benefit of the doubt. Half the people in my bar are regulars and locals. The rest are through here regular enough to live here. Fortune lies not far from a popular travel route to Rathdrum, see. Plenty of folks transporting and peddling need to come through. I already rob them on the poker tables. I don't need to have some stupid drifters pointing a gun in their face for it." Frank let out a long burp. "I have a little thing called *decorum*."

"I'm sorry, Frank . . . I had to ask." He did. Frank was a suspect in this, but in his response, Jesse saw him to be telling the truth. It wasn't the words that sold him. Hell, the man could talk his way around the Devil. Jesse saw the truth in the man's eyes. He saw the hurt in them, the tears forming as he said Christie's name. The fury as he talked of those responsible. There wasn't a hint of guilt in those eyes . . . but there was plenty of pain. "I'd hate to think you think less of me."

"I've had people sling worse at me. But next time you get an idea about speaking your mind about something so ridiculous, wipe your mouth instead." Frank walked over to the door that opened onto the balcony. He looked out its window, arms clasped behind his back. "There's only one thing I care about right now."

"If you're fixin' to put them all in the ground, I'm right there with you, Frank."

"Good," Frank said and beckoned Jesse over as he laid a scrap of paper down on the desk. Jesse looked at the paper. It looked like a crude map. Scrawls of shapes and lines and jottings in handwriting that wasn't much more than a scribble.

"What's that?" Jesse asked.

"That is a map of our murderous friends' ace in the hole," Frank said as he tapped at the yellowing sheet.

"So that's where they're holed up? Where is it?"

"Oswald Mabin's old prospect. A few miles to the northwest toward the mountains."

"The gold mine? I thought Crane owned that?"

Frank nodded. "Correct. Mabin is the man who sold it to him for a bedrock price before he fled. The man knew the place was dry and sought to get out before anyone knew. Always was a slippery son of a gun. Never paid his damned tab." Frank jabbed a finger at the dead man in the chair. "That sorry pecker sang quite a bit once I finally got a tune out of him. Not only did he kindly tell me where they were, but he helped me paint this pretty little picture."

"Now, there's a lot of cover coming in from the forest, so here's where we'll go in." Frank pointed to the scribbles at the bottom of the diagram then moved his finger up toward what looked like awkwardly drawn houses. "Here, between a lot of old carts, buckets and all kinds of junk left behind, are two structures, the head house and the old store. Cullen and his gang are likely to be in either of them because the stamp mill doesn't have much of a roof left." Frank dragged his finger across the map to a much bigger structure with a crude, wonky line drawn through it. "Plenty of cover should it get messy. But I think we can pick them off quiet-like. You got a knife?"

Jesse shook his head. "I've got a gun."

Frank's face soured with disdain. "You better not run out of bullets this time then."

"How many men does Cullen have?"

"According to our dead friend, after last night, eight, including Slim Joe himself."

Jesse whistled. "That's not an easy fight, Frank."

"Which is why we pick them off quiet."

"At night?"

"Oh, no, we hit them this afternoon. They'll hear horses, so we take the last mile on foot. Watch them a while, then pounce."

Jesse stroked at his chin strap beard, which was starting to thicken and spread across his cheeks. He pushed away the thoughts of Christie as he ran through Frank's plan. It didn't feel right. Going quiet wasn't his style. But a head-on collision with eight shooters was a crapshoot with loaded dice.

"Is it just us?" Jesse asked.

"What did I ask you, our first conversation you arrived in Fortune?"

"To help you with Cullen."

"I did that because there's nobody in town that has balls big enough and knows which way to point a gun. They're either cowards or doped up around here. It's just you and me."

"What about your boy Dan?"

"He stays here. Just in case I don't come back."

"You trust him? He can't even talk."

"To people he's got nothing to say to. And that man is like a son to me. He stays."

"Fine." Jesse rubbed at his chin again. "What about the marshals? Can we not get help from them?"

"Sure." Frank shrugged. "If you want to wait six weeks, and by then Cullen will have been back, caught us with our pants down, and finished us off."

"Pinkertons?" Jesse said the name with a grimace. Times were desperate, though.

"If I wanted to waste my money, I'd wheel it down to Cullen now and save us all a lot of trouble. It's me and you, Jesse."

Jesse let out a long sigh. He pinched the bent bridge of his nose as he closed his eyes. A headache crept just behind his ears, a sign he hadn't slept enough.

"All right. I have a different plan, though. One that should get all his men out in the open, keep them contained, and make it less likely we'll get flanked or shot in the back."

"I'm listening."

"How good are you with a Winchester?"

Frank flashed him a predatory grin. "I could de-wing a fly at a hundred yards."

Jesse smiled back at the man. This idea of his might just work.

So long as everything went according to plan.

10

GET YOURSELF KILLED PLAYING THE HERO

Again, Jesse found himself in the cemetery. Standing among the graves, he was staring at a freshly disturbed plot not too far from the nameless sheriff's. Frank was hammering in a wooden cross at the head of it. When the man stood, Jesse could see tears threatening at the corners of his eyes, glistening in the golden late-morning sun.

They'd both gotten a couple hours sleep before they came out to the cemetery at Frank's request to dig out a plot for Christie. It had been short work for the two of them, but to Jesse's tight muscles, it felt long and arduous. Frank just kept digging. He kept at it like a steam engine. He never stopped for breath. He never stopped for a drink. He never said a word the whole time. Seeing him now, Jesse thought he had an idea why. Had he done any of those things, he was apt to break the dam holding back his grief, and that would do them no good right now.

There was work to be done.

There was blood to be spilled.

Retribution to be had.

After the final strike with the hammer, Frank dropped it. He pressed two fingers to his lips then pressed them to the name crudely carved into the wooden crucifix: Christie O'Hanlon. He stood, shoulders slumped, a sad curve in his spine.

"I'm sorry, Christie," whispered Frank. He looked to Jesse, his face gaunt with sorrow. "I'll meet you outside the Jewel when you're ready." He walked away, mindful of the headstones.

"What are you fixin' to do, Jesse Clayton?"

Jesse turned with a start to see Winona standing across the cemetery. She looked tired and a little pale. That didn't detract a bit from her prettiness, though.

"Winona, what are you doing here? You're supposed to be resting. And how'd y—"

"I brought you these back," she said as she thrust out his Stetson and frock coat. Jesse took them and gave her his thanks.

"*Tell me*, Jesse," Winona said, her words and her eyes aflame with fury. "Just what are you and Frank getting ready for?" Winona wasn't a fool. She had a pretty strong idea what it was they had a mind to do. She just wanted to hear him say it.

"What needs to be done," Jesse said flatly.

"I thought that this town wasn't your problem? Huh? You were just passin' through on . . . on the wind, wherever it was takin' you."

"You're right. But then they killed Christie. Who'd done them no harm. And they hurt *you*. Ain't no law around here to make them answer for it. It's up to us to bring them to justice."

"Justice?" Winona laughed and shook her head. "Justice? Killing each other ain't justice. It's just more blood on top of blood. Jesse, come on now, don't get yourself killed when you can just get the right people involved."

"There isn't time, Winona. And I can't let this slide. I won't just walk on when I know there's something I can do about it. I can't live with myself if I move on and then get word down the line that Cullen and his boys struck again and you, or anyone else, is dead because of it. Because of what I *didn't* do."

The fury in her eyes cooled to contempt. Her lips tightened into a frustrated frown and then even that gave out. She sighed and took hold of Jesse's hand.

"Just promise me somethin', Jesse."

"Name it."

"You promise me you'll come back. Don't get yourself killed by playing the hero, okay?"

Jesse took hold of her other hand and brought them together in his. "I'll come back, Winona. I promise." He squeezed them gently. "I need you to promise me something, though."

"What're you wantin' from me?"

There were many things he wanted from her, one of which he wanted, most of all, right then. But even the thought of asking brought the rising in his chest and the stiffness in his jaw. God damn it, he'd killed two men in the night and here he was struggling to talk to a woman without freezing with nerves. "Go—" He had to clear his throat. "Go back to your daddy's ranch."

Her face wrinkled. "Why?"

"It'll be safer for you there. Your daddy has ranch hands, and it's away from here. Should anybody end up in Fortune *if* things go south, my mind will be easier if I know you're out of harm's way. You understand?"

"I guess so," Winona said. She eased her hands out of his.

"Check on my horse for me, too. Haven't forgotten about her."

"All right. I'll do that," Winona said. She put her hands on her hips and said, "But you're coming back... for her, that is."

Jesse laughed as he slipped on his coat. "Yes, indeed. I'm coming back, of course. For her. What's a man to do without his horse?" He smiled at her as he slipped on his hat. "I'll see you soon, Winona."

Winona returned it beautifully. "Goodbye now, Jesse Clayton." She watched as he straightened his Stetson and made for the cemetery exit.

As Jesse walked away, he had a horrible feeling as a thought occurred to him:

What if that was the last time I ever see her smile?

∾

"Thought you might be having second thoughts," said Frank, who stood waiting outside of the Jewel. He was in a fresh shirt and braces, with a holster hanging off his hip. He smoothed out his French mustache and then put on his bowler hat and stepped out in the mud to meet Jesse.

"I've procured us a couple of horses," Frank said. "Now it's just a matter of arming ourselves appropriately. Follow me." He walked over to Wilkerson, who was busy repairing the broken latch on his wagon.

"Ah, gentlemen. To what do I owe the pleasure this fine lunch time?"

"Tobias, I came here for two reasons, to thank you and to ask a favor," Frank said. His tone had that pleasant courteousness a host has when welcoming a guest. Jesse recognized it from his first encounter with the man.

Wilkerson stopped his work and adjusted his spectacles. "But, of course, what can I do you, Mr. Balfour?"

"First, thank you for all your efforts last night and this morning. I'm grateful for you patching up my girls."

"Well." Wilkerson's cheeks bloomed a little. "I merely did what anyone would do . . . were they in a position to help such . . . comely creatures."

"Nevertheless, I thank you all the same, they'll be up and working all-the-sooner because of your endeavors, my friend."

"Well, I—"

Frank continued over him. "Which brings me to the favor I'm about to ask, Tobias, which I don't do lightly. I need ammunition. And I'm gonna need that repeater."

"Oh." Wilkerson said, putting a hand to his chest. "I . . . I can help you with the ammunition, but the repeater, Frank." He paused as if to build up the courage. "I just can't let that go."

Frank grumbled. "Fine. How much?"

"Thirty-five dollars." Tobias squirmed as he said it. "I like you, Frank, and I want to help, but that's the best I can do."

Jesse swallowed. That was a lot of money. Especially in a town like this.

"Okay," Frank said. "How about a counter-offer?"

"I told you Frank I can't go any l—"

"For the bullets and the help last night, I'll wipe your tab. For the Winchester, I'll give you credit to use with the girls and the bar. Deal?"

Wilkerson's eyes widened. "D-d-deal!" He almost squealed the word.

"Excellent," Frank said and then spat in his hand. Wilkerson did the same, and they clasped them together. "Pleasure doing business with you, Tobias, as always."

"The pleasure's all mine, Frank. Really."

"Oh, I know." Frank nodded to Jesse. "If you'll ready the rounds and the rifle for my friend Mr. Clayton here, that would be superb. Thanks again." He turned to Jesse. "I'll go get the horses. You make sure that rifle is as good as advertised."

∼

THEY'D BEEN RIDING a little over an hour when they brought their horses to a stop in the dense thicket. Surrounded by greens and browns and the first dropped leaves of the fall, they tied their mares off to a mossy pine. Jesse took off his frock coat and left it with his horse. He wanted the mobility it would otherwise hinder.

Frank slung the Winchester over his shoulder and pushed rounds into it from a bandolier across his chest as the pair started walking deeper into the woods. The ground had an incline now as they were at the very foot of a mountain. They weren't far from the old Mabin mine now, a mile at most.

"Pretty soon we'll have to be quiet to get the drop on them. You're sure about this plan?" Frank kept his voice low. He carefully chose his steps as they walked through the trees.

"I think it's the best way to account for as many as we can and get 'em out in the open. Less chance of us being ambushed, too," Jesse said, noting that the mud wasn't as deep around here, thanks to the tree cover, no doubt. That would make moving around a lot easier.

"Less chance of *me* being ambushed, you mean. You sure you want to venture in there by yourself?"

"I won't be," Jesse said, keeping an eye on where to plant his foot to avoid the crunch of a leaf. "I'll have you watching my back."

Frank's whispered laugh was a strange thing to hear. "Oh, you've got some balls on you, Clayton."

"As long as you remember my signal and you keep me covered, it should go just fine," Jesse said as a snake slithered past his boot.

"You know, I think I may have forgotten," Frank said. Jesse shot him a look of indifference. Frank mimed a gun with his index finger and thumb and pretended to shoot Jesse. "I've got you covered, Clayton."

11

DIE A FOOL'S DEATH

The old Mabin mine looked like it had seen better days, for sure. The site took up most of the clearing, the trees having been cut down for the space years ago. At the far end, punched into the side of the mountain, was the mine shaft. It was boarded up now, not having been used in years, and the wood looked fragile and discolored from years of rot and weathering.

The site was a mess. Carts and buckets were strewn around between the head house and the store. Those two structures looked relatively intact, though the windows on the front of the store had been broken out. No doubt by somebody looking to steal whatever was left of the wares once for sale there. Jesse had heard about these stores before. When run by the big mining companies, they'd use a credit system that was more apt to trap a man with debt than subsidize his ventures for riches. Perhaps Mabin did the same before he up and abandoned it.

The head house had no windows and was much bigger and therefore the more likely option for the gang to be hiding out. The mill on the other side of the site had half collapsed, like a giant cat all curled in on itself asleep. And with the boards over the mine entrance appearing undisturbed, there wasn't likely to be anyone dwelling down in the dark.

"I'm thinking they're in the head house," Frank said and Jesse wondered if the man was able to read minds. The two of them pressed themselves to neighboring trees, using them and the shade to cover themselves from view.

"I'm inclined to agree with you, Frank," Jesse said. He kept his eyes on the mine, watching for any kind of movement. "You good to shoot from here?"

"No," Frank said. "It's a little too low for my liking. I'm going to make my way around the right flank. So when you draw them out, I can shoot 'em in the back. The ground rises around the tree line up there, too, so I'll have a much better line of sight to cover you."

Jesse nodded slowly. Frank knew what he was doing, and it reassured him. His pulse was steady, but he could feel the adrenaline in him just waiting to be released. The moments preceding a gunfight always had him feeling a little giddy. The mix of fear and anticipation mixed up in Jesse to give him a nervous excitement, butterflies fluttering all crazy-like in his belly.

"You *can* shoot, right, Frank?"

"I know which end the bullets come out, if that's what you're asking." Frank grinned. "I've put many men down with rifles much worse than this when I helped unify this country, son."

Jesse grinned back at him. "All right. Let's do this."

"Every piece of trash down there breathing is an affront to Christie's memory. That gets corrected now," Frank said and turned away, silently making his way up to his vantage point.

Jesse waited a few minutes to give Frank a head start and a chance to get settled in his new position. Last thing he needed was to be too eager and start a fight without backup.

Satisfied he'd waited enough, Jesse kept low and crept out of the tree line, lightly jogging over to the cover of an upturned cart. It was browning at the corners with rust to the point that the metal flaked off at the touch. Jesse silently maneuvered around two more rusting carts and reached a discarded bucket when he froze.

He heard the muffled laughs of multiple men.

Jesse peeked over the bucket slowly. He saw nobody at either the head house or the store. The laugh came again, long and hearty. Jesse clenched his jaw and his fists. Last night these men had set their minds to murder, and now they were laughing and joking like prospectors breaking for lunch. A fresh need for vengeance washed over him as he stepped toward the store.

Jesse came up to the side of the store. It wouldn't do to try and sneak a look in the front and turn his back on the head house. Should somebody come out, he'd be discovered and shot in the back. It would be better to go around the back.

The store was silent as he moved down its left flank to the rear. Reaching the back of it, Jesse hugged the wall and inched toward the doorway, careful to be quiet. The door itself lay in two pieces on the floor. He reached the doorjamb and leaned in slowly, as more of the inside crept into view. Broken shelves, a counter, a few scattered chairs, and some old, broken shovel heads. Thick layers of dust covered everything, and ropey cobwebs lay untouched everywhere.

Nobody here.

The head house it was, then. Jesse walked through the store, paying attention not to disturb any furniture. When a loose floorboard whined, he stopped dead and waited . . . nothing. As nobody had been aroused, he went on to the front entrance. He peered through the broken window just to check it was still clear and then stepped out onto the decking.

The board let out creaking wail just before it collapsed under his foot.

Luckily, his foot only dropped a couple of feet. But it was stuck. He heard a muffled voice from inside the head house say something that sounded a lot like *what the hell was that?* The adrenaline rushed in. Jesse's heartrate picked up, and gooseflesh broke out across his body.

This was *not* part of the plan.

Across from him, the door to the head house burst open and out stepped a man in a familiar-looking filthy duster. One of the Foy twins.

Oh, hell.

Jesse tugged at his foot as he heard Foy shout out to his friends. Finally, the rotted wood gave, and he pulled it out. He jumped down off the deck and onto the mud.

Jesse swiftly assessed his surroundings as the rest of Cullen's men filed out of the house. To his left was an upturned basket that looked like it was mostly rust; it probably wasn't apt to stop a bullet. To his right was a wagon missing a wheel, slumping there like a wounded animal; might could be useful. And there was the cart just down from it he'd used for cover before. If he got the chance, that would be his way out of trouble.

"I thought I'd *kilt* you last night!" Cullen's crude voice boomed as he stepped out. His men had formed a rough line out in the open. All of them had their pistols in their hands. One had a shotgun. Jesse looked up and to his left, glancing at the tree line up on the raised ground and hoping that Frank was where he should be. He was about to put the plan into action a little earlier than anticipated. If Frank wasn't in place, Jesse was about to die a fool's death.

The massive Slim Joe stepped out in front of his crew, chewing on that toothpick again, brandishing his Smith & Wesson casually. "How's it you're still alive?" he asked.

"Your aim's off," Jesse replied with a casual shrug. He kept breathing slowly through his nose. Them having their guns out made this more complicated, too. A false move and Jesse could get real dead real quick. "It's okay, though. It was dark out." Jesse gestured around himself. "It's nice and bright now, at a good range, too. Much fairer this time around . . . for the both of us." Jesse punctuated his words with a wink.

Cullen's men murmured while he rolled that toothpick from one side of his mouth to the other. He forced a laugh. Good, Jesse thought, get him nice and rattled and doubting himself. Keep playing it strong and wait for the moment. He felt sweat begin to bead at the back of his neck.

"That mouth of yours," Cullen said as he lazily pointed his gun in Jesse's general direction, "ain't gonna save you this time, boy."

"You know, I think you're right. I'm just barking at a knot here, aren't I? I'd better just go ahead and shoot you right now, right?"

Cullen laughed. It was heavy, hearty, and horrible to witness. He wiped away spittle from his beard with his sleeve and said, "You reach for that holster, and it'll be the last thing you do, boy."

"You tell 'im, Boss!" yelled one of the Foy twins.

"Shut yer mouth, Dustin, 'fore I shut it for you," Cullen called over his shoulder.

"I didn't mean shoot you with *this* gun," Jesse began as he pointed to his holster. He then slowly looked at his left hand as he raised it. Jesse kept his index finger pointed as he curled in the rest. He kept his thumb up, too, making a gun like a little kid would. "I meant this one."

Cullen's wild eyebrows knitted together, and he grimaced. "Yer gone shoot me with yer damn finger?"

"Nope. But your man on the end there, I will." Jesse aimed his hand at Cullen's man on the left end of the line. "Bang!" Jesse said and threw his arm back, faking the recoil. "Whew! She's got quite the kick!"

Cullen looked at his man, who was very much alive as he patted himself down, and then back at Jesse. He pulled back the hammer on his Smith & Wesson. "Right. Enough. Time to—"

"Hold on a second." Jesse's hand was no longer a gun. Instead, he held up three fingers. "In three . . . two . . . one . . . " At that, he closed his fist and heard the sound of thunder.

The man on the left was flung forward as the bullet punched into the back of his chest. There was another crack of thunder, and another round punched into the mud at Cullen's feet, sending up a geyser of mud.

"Cover!" he yelled as he ran for the safety of the head house. As Frank rained down more thunderous shots from his Winchester repeater, Cullen's men scattered, some hugging the wall of the head house, others scrambling in the mud for whatever cover they could find.

Jesse was behind the wagon now, Colt drawn and ready. He wanted nothing more than to cheer for that volley of shots from Frank. Jesse leaned out from the downed wagon and aimed his Colt at a man who was taking cover behind a cart. He had his back to Jesse as he was firing in Frank's direction. Jesse pulled the trigger and the man cried out and sagged into the cart, his revolver clanging as it bounced off it.

This drew the others' attention. They spun and fired at Jesse. He blindly returned two shots before ducking back behind the wagon. He thumbed open the loading gate and swiftly replaced the spent bullets. He heard one of Cullen's men attempt a flanking tactic, but as he hopped out of the safety of cover, Frank's rifle boomed again, and he flew face first into the mud.

Jesse leaned out and caught sight of another shooter, this one in a brown trilby hat, leaning out of the side of a downed bucket. Frank wouldn't be able to clip him from there, but Jesse could. He swiftly dropped to one knee and brought up his Colt, steadying his wrist with his free hand. He inhaled, then squeezed the trigger as he held his breath. The man's trilby flew off as his head snapped back and his body went limp. Another salvo of bullets forced Jesse back behind the cart again. This time, he kept snug to it as he darted to the other end, then dashed across and rounded the upturned cart and ducked behind it.

"STOP IT! STOP IT NOW!" Cullen bellowed and the shooting stopped. "He's got help up in them trees up there. Foys, you two go on and take care o' that shooter he got in the trees! Tanner, you're with me. We gone go either side of that wagon and cut him in two."

Well, it took them longer than he thought it would to figure out, Jesse thought, but they'd finally cottoned to it, and this was where things would get tricky. Thankfully, their numbers had been thinned a fair bit. Jesse was confident he could take those two. He just hoped Frank would be okay dancing with the Foy twins.

He heard them all go their separate ways, then the oncoming squelching of the pair who had designs on killing him. Jesse backed away from the cart and to the back of the store. Tanner saw him as he got to the rear of the store and opened fire, blowing chunks of wood and dust from the corner of it over Jesse.

Jesse entered the store and backed up to the wall on his right, keeping his gun trained on the entrance as he heard the sluggish squelching of boots struggling through mud. That became the sound of thumping on wood as Tanner—no way he figured Cullen could move that fast—got onto the decking.

Jesse didn't even wait until he could see the man, just judged it from the sound and fired three rounds through the rotting wood wall. Tanner let out a yelp, and a second later Jesse saw him hit the floor across the rear entrance. He was looking at Jesse, his face a picture of pain and rage. He still had his weapon and was using what little life he had left to raise—

Jesse fired again and Tanner was still.

Just Cullen left now. But where was he? Jesse tried to focus his hearing but the reports of gunfire in the distance and the ringing in his ears from his own shooting made that difficult.

Frank must have his hands full, too.

Jesse tried to guess Slim Joe's next move. He had to know that Tanner was lying dead out back. Cullen was dumb, sure, but he knew how to fight and how to fight *dirty,* too, most likely. He'd be waiting with a line of sight on one of those exits, ready to shoot Jesse down the moment he stepped into the warm light of the afternoon.

The question was: which one was it? It was a gamble Jesse wasn't particularly keen on making, given that he'd surely used up all his luck already these past couple days in Fortune. He could feel his heartrate rising and breathed deep and slow; he wrinkled his nose as he took in the stale and fusty odor of the store.

He made up his mind. He would—

The wall behind him burst inward and he was thrown forward into the shelves opposite. They snapped, dousing him in dust and cobwebs. He coughed and hacked as he tried to regain his composure. He turned and raised his Colt but something huge slapped his hand and he lost it. He heard it clatter somewhere in the store. Two plate-sized hands grabbed him by the scruff of his neck and lifted him off the ground. He felt hot, rancid breath on his face.

Jesse was slammed into the wall. He cried out as he felt something give in his chest. He cried as he was slammed again and again. He was carried across the room and slammed into the other wall, before he was launched across the store, crashing into the counter, which disintegrated under him.

Slowly, he pushed himself off the floor. He blinked, but his eyes wouldn't focus. His ears were ringing louder than ever. Pain racked his body, and he could taste copper. Those big hands seized him again as he heard a barbaric chuckle from Cullen.

Sluggishly, Jesse reached out, grasping at anything he could lay his fingers on as Cullen lifted him to his feet. His hands closed around something wooden, and he spun like a viper and swung it at Cullen, who ducked his head and leaned his arm into the blow. The wood shattered across him. Jesse didn't stop. He threw a punch into Cullen's abdomen, who stumbled back slightly and threw a right hook that cracked Jesse's jaw. He staggered with the blow. He brought up his left hand and—

Cullen grabbed his wrist with a meaty hand. He planted one punch into Jesse's torso, and Jesse wheezed as the wind flew out of him. He panted and huffed for a breath that wouldn't come. Cullen then dealt him a blow to the side of his face and stars bloomed across his vision. His eyesight became awfully unsteady.

"You know, you've got some fight in you, boy," Cullen said. The big man took a step back and let his breathing settle. "After a few blows like that, most men would be down and out. You can't throw a punch but you sure can *take* one. I like that. But I'm gonna beat you into the dirt now. You'll watch the lights go out, right before your lungs fill up with that thick, soupy mud." Cullen let out a menacing chuckle. The man was laughing, and Jesse was just trying to stay on his feet. "Normally, I'd just put a bullet in yer. But you made fools of my boys. You made a fool of *me*. And then you came here to kill me." He chuckled again. "As if you could. I'm Slim Joe *Goddamn* Cullen, ya hear?" He rammed a fist into Jesse's abdomen, and this time he dropped to his knees. He put out his hands to stop himself going prone.

Cullen grabbed his hair, and as Jesse tried his best not to scream, he wondered when he'd lost his hat. Once he was upright, Cullen took him by the scruff again and carried him out of the shack. As the sunlight washed over him, Jesse felt a brief moment of peace. Then he was aware of the warm torrent that was oozing from his left eyebrow, the teeth that suddenly felt loose, the agony in his stomach, his ribs and his lungs. Two of his fingers hurt something fierce, too.

Cullen tossed him and Jesse hit the mud, sliding a few yards across the viscous muck. Cullen walked over to him and delivered a swift boot into Jesse's side, causing him to roll over on to his back with a wheezing groan.

This is it.

Jesse sluggishly moved his legs, dragged them through the mud trying to find purchase. They just kept sliding to no avail. He couldn't get up. He pushed on his hands, but they wouldn't take his weight. His strength had been beaten out of him. He thought of the man In Fortune clutching his face as he'd done the same.

No. No, it can't be.

Slim Joe Cullen laughed and stooped over him. "I know that look," he said. "I've seen that look before. It's the fear in the eyes . . . *that's* the giveaway. That is the look of a man who knows that he is not long for God's earth and there isn't a damned thing he can do about it."

Not like this. Please.

He wouldn't say the words. He wouldn't give Cullen the satisfaction. Honestly, he probably couldn't anyway.

Cullen dropped to his knees and straddled Jesse. He put a meaty hand on the side of Jesse's face and started to push. "You hear that?" he said, looking around. "It's gone awful quiet. That means your shooter friend ain't around no more. My boys will be back any minute with him. He'll probably be dead . . . but I hope he isn't. I'd really like to do to him what I'm about to do to *you*."

Please. No.

"Make your peace with God, if you're that way inclined, as I am about to send you to the next world." Cullen rolled that toothpick in his mouth as he cracked his knuckles.

He could feel the coolness of the mud as it slowly rose up to meet him. It swallowed his cheek, and he closed his eye as that sank in, and pursed his lips as the corner of his mouth reached it. He raised his arms and sluggishly swiped at Cullen. The man simply leaned his head back and chuckled. The world was darkening. His nose was lost to the mud now, his remaining eye darting feverishly in its socket. Jesse took one last breath as the world went dark.

Winona, I'm sorry.

His lungs started to burn.

∼

SOMETHING FELL ON HIM. Something heavy. His lungs were on fire now. All he wanted to do was inhale, but he knew to do that meant death. He tried to lift his head, but he was stuck too deep. The mud was too strong. His arms were pinned, too. He squirmed and struggled with what little fight he had left.

Suddenly, that huge weight was lifted from him. He felt something burrowing around his head. He saw a glimpse of light. His lungs! His lungs burned with a fury he had never felt. He had to open his mouth. He couldn't fight it any—

He took a deep breath and expected to take in a lungful of soupy mud. Instead, his lungs took in air. He gasped, then coughed a sickly, hacking wretch. He felt the sunlight on his face again, the sensation of his head rising, something pawing at his face, squeezing his nose, and digging in his ears.

"Jesse?" He heard a voice. Echoey and muffled and yet familiar. "Jesse, can you hear me?"

Jesse opened his eyes and saw Frank. He tried to say his name, but all he could do was desperately gasp for breath. Frank pulled him up to a sitting position and gave him a few minutes until he could speak. He looked around and saw Slim Joe sprawled next to him, clutching his guts, groaning, and wincing. Jesse then looked down at his hands and saw that two of the fingers on his right hand were facing the wrong way. That would explain the pain.

"They're just dislocated," Frank said. "Saw them as I was pullin' you out. I can pop them back in for you if you want."

"Please," Jesse wheezed.

"It'll hurt like hell."

Jesse offered his hand. Frank took the two fingers and Jesse looked away. Frank jerked the fingers back into place with a pop and Jesse felt a searing rush of white-hot pain that brought on a fresh rise of nausea. This time he screamed.

"Thank you, Frank," Jesse said at last and flexed his fingers. "I thought I was dead."

"If anything, it's my sense of timing you should thank. He had you sunk up to your shoulders when I got here. 'Course, I didn't realize 'til after I'd put the bullet through his belly."

Jesse looked at Cullen. Despite the pain, he still gripped that toothpick between his bloodied teeth. And he wasn't sure why, but that little piece of wood irritated him more than a little.

Jesse struggled to his feet, and Frank handed him his hat and his colt, saying that he'd found them in the store. "Was it always that much of a mess, or did you two tango in there?" Frank asked.

"Cullen decided to redecorate . . . used me to do it."

"Ouch."

"I tend to fight a little better with this," Jesse said as he held up his Colt. He looked at it and saw that the barrel was blocked with mud. He frowned at it. He didn't have any gear to clean it out here.

Frank hummed in agreement. "If only you'd had something like a knife to level the playing field," Frank said as if to himself. Then he looked over at Cullen. "What do you want to do with him?"

"I say we leave him for the wolves."

"Aw, come on now. No need for that," Cullen said and groaned again.

"You know how to get mud out of a gun?" Jesse asked Frank, ignoring Cullen's plea.

"Let me look," Frank said, and Jesse handed him the hand cannon. "Ah, I know just what to do." He aimed the gun at Cullen and fired it twice. Cullen howled as mud and bullets spat from the barrel, striking him in both legs. Frank then inspected the barrel before handing it back to Jesse. "All clear."

Jesse watched the man who'd nearly just killed him writhe in fresh pain and saw that now the toothpick had fallen from his mouth onto his shirt. Only, it was more like half of a toothpick; one end was all ragged from being chewed.

Sheepishly, as he was still a little woozy from his beating and near suffocation, Jesse staggered over to the still howling Cullen and plucked the toothpick off his chest.

Frank whistled to him, and Jesse turned around.

"Come on," Frank said. "There's a stream nearby you can wash the rest of that mud off before we get going. If we're quick, we can be back before dusk." Jesse nodded and followed him, slipping the toothpick into his pocket.

The pair of men kept walking as the moans of a dying man slowly faded.

∼

JESSE DUNKED his head in one last time and felt the cool crispness of the water give him a fresh sense of vigor and vitality. Then he raked his hair back as best he could with his fingers and then joined Frank, who was holding the horses.

"So, what will you do now this is all over?" Frank asked him, chewing a piece of jerky.

"I'm not sure this is over, Frank."

Frank raised his dark eyebrows. "My, you *were* in that mud a long time."

"I'm serious."

"Cullen's dead. And so's his gang, almost. The two that came after me turned tail and ran the moment I fired on them. Straight for their horses and gone. It's over, Jesse, and I thank you for it.

You've shown yourself to be a man to ride the river with. In my book, anyways."

"Look at this, Frank." Jesse showed him Cullen's chewed toothpick.

He turned his nose up at it and shrugged. "The man liked a toothpick. So what?"

Jesse reached into his pocket again and produced another one. "These two look the same to you?" He asked Frank. Balfour looked at the second pick, then the first again and then nodded with satisfaction.

"I got this second one from Sullivan Crane's house."

That stopped Frank mid-chew.

"I was in his office, and it was on the floor, right next to the chair I was sitting in, Frank."

Frank threw the jerky on the floor and walked to his horse. "You know, Jesse, I'm thinking that this isn't over."

12

DELIVER JUSTICE WITH THE PULL OF A TRIGGER

They reached the estate just as the sun was on the decline; dusk was not far off. The air had grown cool with the evening wind, and the first of the crickets were beginning their stridulations. The pair of them dismounted and walked up to the steps of the mansion, which was all lit up with lanterns.

Frank whistled as he looked upon the huge house. "Is it as good on the inside as it looks on the outside?"

"Depends on your taste," Jesse said.

Three men, one of whom Jesse recognized as Crane's bodyguard, Brad, came down the steps to meet them. Two of them had their hands on their hips. Brad was holding a shotgun.

"Can I help you, gentlemen?" Brad asked, his face just as serious as before.

"Brad! Good to see you again," Jesse said cheerfully. "Just here to talk to Mr. Crane, shouldn't take too long."

"Mr. Crane is not taking visitors tonight. I'm sorry, but you'll just have to turn around and go."

Jesse sighed. "Now, Brad, I understand you're just doing your job, but I need you to understand somethin' here." Jesse started to tick off fingers on his good hand. "I'm very tired. I am in a lot of pain. I do not have the patience for this wonderful to-and-fro we're about to have . . . so how's about we just go ahead and skip to the part where you let us on by."

"What business do you have with Mr. Crane, exactly?"

"The kind that has about as much to do with you as a bar of soap," Frank interjected.

Brad tightened his grip on the shotgun.

Jesse waved him off. "Thank you, Frank. Very helpful." He then pointed his finger slowly at the scattergun. "Don't. Just don't. I don't have the tolerance for this, Brad. Not tonight. Not after the day I've had. We throw down, we're not all walking away, and then it's up to the marshals or the Pinkertons to pick up the pieces and put together how this all went down. Whichever gets here first."

Brad was taken aback. "Pinkertons? Law's coming?"

Jesse nodded. "It's why I'd like to be done here quick. Now, I'm sure you're all just men looking to make money, but depending on how you stand now, you can either be on the side of the law or end up wrapped up in what trouble is coming your boss's way. Easy enough to just step aside, then collect what you're owed once we're done and leave."

"How we gonna take our pay from a dead man?"

"Not here to kill him and we ain't goin' to, are we, Frank?"

Frank said nothing.

"Are we, *Frank*?"

"No," he said at last, then added coldly, "He'll still be alive once we're through with him."

Brad eyeballed them for a moment. Then he gave them a curt nod and stepped aside. He motioned for his men to do the same. Jesse and Frank nodded back and ventured up the steps.

"Twenty minutes. Then we come in."

"You got it," Jesse called back. "That's plenty enough. Thank you!"

"My God," Frank whispered back as they got to the door. "Marshals and Pinkertons? Where'd you come up with that manure?"

"You know, it just *came* to me," Jesse said smugly.

"You're just slick enough to slip the devil, aren't you?"

"Sure beats having to shoot people," Jesse said and pushed through the big doors.

∼

THE DOWNSTAIRS WAS EMPTY, save for the housekeeping staff. As they'd gone room to room, Jesse had heard Frank's utterances of surprise. Clearly, the inside was as impressive as Frank had wondered on their arrival.

Meeting back in the foyer, they made for the stairs.

"The man lives in a damn palace, and he spends his nights in the Jewel? What's wrong with him?" Frank said.

"Maybe he just gets lonely, living in a big house like this."

A housemaid was awaiting them at the top of the stairs. Her apron was immaculate, and she stood with a smile, but her eyes betrayed her fear.

"It's okay, ma'am. We're not here to do harm," Jesse said, keeping his hands wide and away from his hips.

"Mr. Crane is waiting for you in his office, if you'll follow me, gentlemen," she said in a pleasant, if shaky, voice. She spun on her heel and walked across the landing. Jesse and Frank followed without a word until they came to a familiar set of doors.

The housemaid pushed open the doors and then stood to the side. The two men entered and approached the desk, on the other side of which Sullivan Crane sat in his chair in a bright white suit. His bulbous cheeks bore the smoothness of a fresh shave, and one of them now sported an unsightly bruise: big, purple, and yellowing at the edges. He held a cigar, and its smoke hung above him like a dark cloud threatening rain. Or worse.

"Good evening, gentlemen. I have to say I wasn't expecting a visit at this hour," Crane said. He looked at Jesse's face and his mug took on a mask of shock. "Heavens! What happened to your face?"

"Cullen happened," Frank said simply. "Then we happened to him. Him and his gang aren't going to trouble Fortune anymore."

"Well . . . well that's great news!" Crane almost choked the words out. "I heard what happened last night after I left the Jewel, and I have to say, my condolences to you, Frank, from the bottom of my heart. And to you, Jesse. I do hope that Miss Squires makes a swift and complete recovery. I myself am still feeling the affects of his assault on my person prior." He rubbed at the purple patch on his face.

"Cut the crap, Sullivan," Frank spat. "I'm not here for your lies."

"What on earth are you talking about, Frank?" Crane replied, sounding puzzled. Or attempting to.

"Come on, Sullivan. Come clean," Jesse began. "Do I really need to spell it out for you?"

"I have no idea what it is you're referring to, Mr. Clayton. And quite frankly, I am not fond of the tone you're taking."

"Fine. I'll spell it out. I found a few things right off with you my first day in town. Your insistence on buying up property in a town that's all but dead. The need for not one but two bodyguards, who happened to not be around on both occasions that Cullen and his boys struck the town. A coincidence the first time. But twice? Uncanny."

"And for my folly I was assaulted by that foul beast of a man!"

"Could have easily been for show. Hell, if I were him, I probably would have done that even without your say-so. What could you do? Nothing without showing your hand to everybody in that saloon. Nope, you take your hidin' like a good boy and play along. But it all made sense when we finally caught up to Cullen up at the Mabin's old gold mine, which, if I'm not mistaken, you now own, am I right?"

Crane sat silent. His face was taut with anger.

"Once we'd put a bullet in him, which was easy enough, I got this off of him." Jesse flung the bloody and chewed toothpick onto Crane's desk. "Which is really interesting, because it looks awful similar to this . . ." Jesse threw the other toothpick onto the desk. ". . . which I happened upon in this very office the day before. Is *that* a coincidence?"

"Well, would you look at that," Frank said and bent down. When he came back up, he was holding another one, all chewed up on one end. "Here's another." He flung it at Crane, who flinched as it hit his chest.

"This is preposterous. What you're suggesting is ludicrous. Nothing more than hearsay and happenstance!" Crane protested.

Jesse nodded and smiled despite the pain. Only one side of his mouth lifted, mind you. "That's true. It wouldn't stand up in the eyes of the law. It's a good job we've got Slim Joe himself back in town. And he is fit and ready to sing like a bird about all the work he's done for you . . . particularly how you ordered the attack on the Jewel."

He shot up from the desk. "I never said to *kill* anyone!" Crane's fury melted away into regret as he realized his folly. He sank back into his chair. "I said to cause a scene. It was *you*, Clayton. You got him all riled up."

"Well, that's good to know," Jesse said. "And I'm glad you admitted it because we actually left Joe gut-shot and bleedin' out up at your mine. If he ain't dead, he sure will be soon. Hopefully, before the wolves get scent of him, for his sake."

Crane grumbled something under his breath that Jesse could not make out.

"I'd apologize for the trickery, but in light of what's transpired because of you, I'm sure it can be forgiven. I just wanna know, because I cannot figure it out myself—why?"

"You wouldn't figure it out, you small-minded drifter."

"Are we killing this goddamned weasel or what?" Frank said, eyeballing Crane with flames in his eyes.

"No!" Crane bleated. "You can't. If you kill me, you kill Fortune!"

"I look like I give a crap, Sullivan?" Frank pulled out his gun.

"Look, just wait. Wait! Jesse, tell him, please!" Crane's voice had risen a whole octave. "You can't kill me for the very reason I did all this: To keep Fortune alive! N-not only that, but to make it prosperous again, you see? E-even more so than it was during the boom of the mine. I bought that mine for a reason. Not because I thought there was gold, but because it was surrounded by something so much more valuable."

"The trees," Jesse said.

"Yes! Lumber is something every prospector, rancher, or whatever will need going forward, and this town is surrounded by it. That mine is the perfect place to set up a lumber yard! And it will put Fortune on the map again!"

"Not really," Frank said. "Fortune doesn't exactly have the greatest of roads. And what's it near to? Rathdrum's the closest, and it's miles away."

Suddenly, Crane had grown confident. The pleading tone had disappeared from his voice. He sounded like a man about to play the ace up his sleeve. "I have been in contact with agents from the railway. In a few days, they're coming to town to meet me so I can make this deal. They'll bring the railroad to Fortune, and we can rail the lumber across the country."

"And if we kill you . . . we kill the deal," Jesse said.

"Absolutely," Crane said as he leaned back in his chair. A smugness occupied his face as he took a pull on his cigar. "You fools think you can ride up in here and deliver justice with a pull of a trigger? That's not how things work in business, gentlemen. Money is what makes the world go around."

"You son of a bitch!" Frank said. "Christie had to die so you and your bigshot railway pals can turn a profit?" Frank shot forward, skirted the big desk and pressed the barrel of his gun into Crane's forehead. The fat man squealed.

"Frank, no!" Jesse yelled.

"This wasn't about saving Fortune." Frank got into Crane's personal space. "It's about money. That's all it's ever been about. That's why you've been buying up as much real estate as you can. You know once that iron horse starts rolling through here, this town will blow up and so will the value of every square inch of property." Frank twisted his gun slowly as Crane closed his eyes. The mayor was a terrified, sweaty mess. "You've squeezed every cent you can out of these people as you've undersold them. and then when that didn't work, that's when you called in your dog Cullen. Is that about right?"

Crane said nothing, only cowered with his eyes closed.

"*Is that right?*" Frank growled and pressed the barrel deeper.

Crane's cheeks jiggled as he nodded furiously.

"Frank," Jesse said softly. "Shooting him might make you feel better. But it won't bring Christie back. But this way you can help a lot of people."

"All I see us doing by keeping him alive is helping him turn blood into cash." Frank's hand was shaking now. "I won't do it."

"That won't happen, Frank. Because this is what's gonna happen instead. Sullivan, you're gonna call a town meeting when those train folks get here, so you can publicly announce the railroad to the town. Even make the signing public, whatever. Point is, the town knows about it. Then you're gonna give back the property to anyone who still lives in town. I mean give, not sell back. Give. Call it reparations. And anyone in town who needs a home, or a job, they're your new workforce for this lumber yard and they get paid starting next week, whether that yard is up or not. Understand?"

Crane nodded.

"That good for you, Frank?"

"No. But it's a *start*." He pulled the gun away from Crane's forehead. It had left a mark that would leave another bruise.

"I guess that's that, then," Jesse said. "We'll leave you to start organizing that, Mayor." Jesse turned and started for the door.

"Just one more thing," Frank said. He aimed his pistol at Sullivan's shin and pulled the trigger. Jesse jumped at the sound and the mayor howled and clutched his leg. He began to call out for help as Frank joined Jesse.

They were halfway downstairs when Brad and the guards came running up, weapons raised. Jesse and Frank raised their hands and stepped aside.

"We said we wouldn't *kill* him," Frank said.

∼

ATOP OF THEIR HORSES, Jesse and Frank trotted down the lane away from Sullivan's estate.

"A drink at the Jewel on our return, a toast to justice?" Frank asked.

"Think I'll take a rain check on that one, Frank," Jesse said. "Winona's ranch ain't but two whoops and a holler from here. I might head there, check that she's okay and pick up my horse."

"Fair enough." He extended his hand, which Jesse shook. "We make quite the team. I suppose I'll see you tomorrow."

"Goodbye, Frank, and thank you for watching my back."

"And for saving your life." And at that, Frank tugged at the reins of his horse and took off into the dying light of dusk.

13

ENOUGH BLOOD'S BEEN SPILLED

Jesse rode up to the ranch and knew immediately that something was amiss. Light emanated from inside the house, casting long shadows around it. He couldn't see his horse tied off where he'd left her. He looked around from his position down the road and spied no movement in the windows downstairs, but there did seem to be activity up in one of the bedrooms.

Once he reached the house, Jesse felt a knot in his stomach, and he suddenly forgot the pain and the fatigue. He could see his horse now. She was where he'd left her, only she was lying on the ground in a pool of blood and dirt. He slid off the horse, wary he might have already alerted anyone to his presence and quietly hurried to the wall of the house.

He listened a moment and heard a voice inside talking. It sounded irritated, but he could not discern what was being said. He would need to get a look in there. Keeping himself pressed to the farmhouse wall, Jesse sidled over to the nearest window. Slowly, like he'd done in the abandoned store at the mine, he eased his head over little by little to gain a look inside.

It was the living room, and the table where he'd patched up Bill Squires was now overturned. A man that Jesse didn't recognize was tied to a chair, his head all bloodied. He must have been the ranch hand Bill had working the place. Jesse inched farther over to widen his angle of view. Now, he saw old Bill himself, also bound to a chair and looking in even sorrier state than his hired hand. Somebody stepped in front of him—in a familiar tattered duster.

George Foy.

It made sense. Frank had put the fear of God into the Foy brothers with the demonstration of the repeating rifle, leaving them no recourse but to flee. Their time in Fortune was now done, and they were apt to be fending for themselves a while. They'd need money to tide them over. Why not finish what they started on a lonely road a couple nights ago? Pretty clever for a pair of brothers who had more fingers than they could count.

That meant Dustin was upstairs. And he wouldn't be alone. The realization of what could be happening to Winona meant that Jesse's window of opportunity to act shrank considerably. Every moment he wasted, she was closer to harm. And he was not about to let that happen. He made his mind up quickly.

He'd be neighborly about it.

Jesse stepped up to the front door and rapped on it three times. He then stepped to the side and drew his Colt. Inside, the irritated whining of George Foy had stopped. Footsteps plodded up to the door, and then it opened.

Jesse shoved the barrel of his Colt into George's neck and put a finger to his lips.

"Good evening, George. Nice to see you again. Now, don't go callin' out, I'd hate to be spooked into pulling the trigger here. You understand? Blink twice if you do."

George blinked twice.

Jesse gave instructions and George followed them to the letter. First, they backed up into the house, and with his opposite hand he drew his gun from his holster and handed it over. Jesse locked eyes with Bill, whose sullen demeanor perked up mightily upon seeing him.

His plan went sideways as Dustin came down the stairs. "She ain't talkin'. We'll just take turns on her then run with the money—" He stopped as he saw his brother and Jesse. Immediately, he retreated up the stairs.

Oh, hell.

Jesse heard screams from Winona and shouts from Dustin and the bumps and bangs of a struggle.

"Winona!" Jesse called up the stairs. "It's all right. Don't fight. I'm here and I'm gonna see you safe, you hear? Don't fight him, he ain't gonna do you any harm." George struggled and Jesse jammed the barrel into his neck. "Stop that, or this bullet'll be comin' out of your ear."

"And then your girlie will die."

"You figured that out all by yourself? Well, George, I'm impressed. I think you and your brother can get out of this alive if you start listenin'."

"You ain't gonna let us live."

"I will. As long as Winona's unharmed, I don't see why you can't just up and leave and none of us see each other again."

"Really?"

"I'm shootin' straight, George. I'm tired, and I'd really like to get some sleep. You just gotta help me talk sense to your brother."

Two sets of footsteps came down the stairs, and after a few seconds, Winona came into view, a gun pressed to her temple. Her figure was swallowed up by a white nightgown; blotches of blood dotted the front of it. Her lip was cut, bloody and swollen. But otherwise, she looked okay. She walked calmly as Dustin pressed himself behind her, using her as a shield much in the way Jesse was using George. The two of them stopped at the bottom of the stairs.

"You okay, Winona?" Jesse asked.

"I'm fine."

"Both of you, shut up!" Dustin said. He looked like he hadn't slept in days, and like he had even fewer teeth than the other night. "Now, Jesse Clayton. How do you oppose we get out of this problem?"

"Suppose," Jesse corrected.

"Pardon me?"

"You know what, it doesn't matter. As I was saying to your brother here." Jesse patted George on the shoulder. "He and I are real pals now, by the way. How about we solve this nice and peaceful? You give me Winona, I give you back your brother and you both and just up and walk out of here with whatever you've taken. And none of us ever see each other again."

Dustin's top lip drew back, and his eyes narrowed.

"Ain't that right, George?" Jesse said. "Go on, tell him."

"Y-yeah, Dustin, it's what he done said to me. And I believe him."

Dustin's look of contemplation was as ugly as a mud fence. Seconds ticked by as he considered the offer. As he did, Jesse spied Winona's hands steadily sliding across her belly to meet one another. He looked her in the eye and shook his head almost imperceptibly. She nodded back in a similarly discreet way.

"Say I was to agree, how would we go about that?" Dustin said.

"It's easy. We both put our guns away and then step aside. And you and your brother here walk on out, never to be seen again."

Winona's hand slipped up the cuff of her gown. Her derringer dropped into her left hand. Jesse applied pressure to George's neck, forcing his gaze up and away from Winona's doings.

"Nope. Don't like it. Ain't no way I'm dropping this iron. I saw what you did at the gold mine. And if you're here now, that means you put down Slim Joe, too."

"You're right, I did. And I'm thinking enough blood's been spilled by my hand for one day," Jesse said as he watched Winona slowly move her hand behind her.

"I don't care. You put your gun down and we walk out. Only way this works."

"I can't do that, Dustin."

"Well what d'you say then?"

Jesse sighed heavily. "I'm sorry, Dustin."

An ugly look of confusion took Dustin's face as the derringer went off. He staggered back and took aim in reaction, firing off a round of his own. His bullet caught George in the chest. He gasped as it struck him. George fell into Jesse, who had to drop his gun to catch him.

Jesse watched George's sad and pained face as he said, "Dustin? Dustin why'd . . . why'd you shoot me?"

Dustin dropped his gun, and it clattered across the floor. He slumped against the wall. He coughed up blood as he slid to the floor, leaving a smear of blood on the wall. His head lolled. He looked like a drunk sleeping off a snout full.

Jesse held George in his arms. He felt George's grasping fingers lose their grip on his forearms as his breath became all patchy and erratic. "Why would . . . you shoot me . . . Dustin?" He asked again. He spasmed and Jesse held him firm, whispering to him that he was sorry. That George was going to be okay and that he was sorry. George's voice became more subdued now. "Why . . . Dustin? I'm . . . I'm . . . your brother." George exhaled one last time.

He never spoke again.

～

IT WAS AN HOUR LATER. Jesse and Winona had freed up the ranch hand and her father, and together they had moved the bodies out of the house. A decision was made to cover them up, then take them to town in the morning for a proper burial. They may not have been good men, but they at least deserved better than the indignity of being buried in an unmarked grave in a livestock grazing field.

Sitting with Bill and Winona, Jesse went through a shortened version of all that had happened after the attack on the Jewel: the showdown with Cullen and his men (Jesse may have omitted certain details of how the fight with him had gone.), and the revelation of Crane's involvement and the likely arrival of the railway in Fortune.

"Well, I'll be," Bill said as he rocked back in his chair. "I never did trust Crane. He's run a lot of good folks out of this town. Can't say I'm too happy with Frank, either, with him only shooting him in the leg. I'd have been inclined to put that bullet in his fat head. Got off too easy, in my book."

"And Fortune would have died along with him," Winona pointed out. "He's the only one that can land that railway deal."

Jesse nodded. "You're right. And he's putting together a timber industry that would be big enough to get Fortune well back on its feet again."

"I guess you're right. Funny, I remember you tellin' me you were just passing through." Bill chuckled. He stood up and clapped Jesse on the shoulder. "Besides, you look like you've gone through the mill. Get some yourself some sleep, son. You got eyes redder'n the devil. Goodnight."

Jesse looked over at Winona, who said, "He's got a point."

"Lead the way," Jesse said.

∽

JESSE LAY on Winona's bed, shirtless and bootless. The mattress was thin and stiff but to him it was the most comfortable thing he'd lain on in what felt like forever. It was easier to count the parts of him that didn't hurt, he realized as he lay there assessing how rough he felt. Fortuitously, nothing was broken, he didn't think. Just mightily bruised. He hoped anyway. He reckoned he'd just see how bad he felt in the morning.

"I didn't need your help, you know," Winona said. She was lying on her side next to him, her head propped up on one hand.

"Sure, you didn't," Jesse replied. "You had it all under control upstairs in the bedroom."

"That's where my derringer was. I needed to get it. I was playing along at getting him money and I was gonna use it on him until you showed up actin' like a hero."

"I'm real sorry about that."

Winona frowned at him. Of course, Jesse couldn't see this as he had his eyes closed. He could feel the idea of sleep tugging at the corners of his mind. He didn't see her lean in closer to him, either.

"All you managed to do was talk a lot of ballyhoo and then almost get yourself shot. I don't see how much help you were at all, really."

"Well," Jesse said and then immediately yawned, bringing fresh pain across his injured jaw. "I am infinitely grateful for your actions that not only saved you and your father, but also me from my foolishly rash decision that almost jeopardized your grand plan."

"Oh, shut up," Winona said and nudged him. After a pause she said, "You know, there's a way to show me *how* grateful you are."

Jesse didn't respond.

Winona nudged him again. "Jesse?"

Still no response.

"*Hey!*"

Jesse started to snore.

14

A RED-LETTER DAY

Five Days Later

"And with this deal, today, the fortunes of Fortune will be forever changed for the *better*!" Sullivan Crane's booming words carried across the street as he addressed the crowd in the middle of Main Street, "Today, this town rises from the ashes."

Jesse Clayton stood with Frank Balfour on the balcony of his office at the Jewel, watching the speech with great interest. He sipped a cup of coffee that was strong enough to float a Colt and almost too bitter to swallow. Frank seemed to enjoy it just fine.

So far, they'd liked what they'd heard. The railway was coming to Fortune. Well, it was actually about half a mile away, but there would be a station by the name of *Fortune, Idaho*. That was thanks to the two bespectacled bigshots on Crane's left, standing in suits even fancier than his. Crane was right after all. There *was* money to be made on the back of the iron horse.

"In a few weeks," Sullivan continued, "my new lumber yard will open at the old site of the Mabin mine. It will be the beginning of a new age of prosperity in Fortune. And I offer the guarantee of a job at that site to any man that needs one. Pay will be fair. And they will be part of this town's great resurrection."

"My, my." Frank said over his coffee cup. "The man loves the sound of his own voice, doesn't he?"

"Come on, Frank. Let him have it."

"I should have let him have that bullet to his fat head instead of his shin."

Down in the street, Crane continued, "'Why?' you ask. The answer to that is quite simple, ladies and gentlemen: the best way . . . the *only* way to rebuild this town . . . is together." Crane paused as a couple in the crowd whooped and cheered. "No longer will they say that Fortune favors the dead. One day, in the very near future, they will say that Fortune favors any who come here. Thank you and good morning!"

The moment he finished the crowd erupted into applause.

"Can you hear that?" Frank said.

"The sound of a new beginning?"

"Nope. The sound of a lot of happy people about to spend a lot of money on booze and whores. It's a red-letter day for Fortune. That's good for business."

Jesse smiled wryly. "People gotta celebrate somehow, I guess."

Once the applause died down the crowd broke up. As people started to amble home (or to the Jewel, as most of them did) the two of them watched as Crane actually put his cane to use, limping with the pair of railway men over to the hotel, two of his bodyguards in tow.

"I won't ever get tired of seeing that limp," Frank said and slung the dregs of his coffee into the street, and then perched an elbow on the railing, leaning against it. "So, what will you do now?" he asked. "You came here wanting nothing to do with us. Then helped turn this place around in a matter of days. So what's next for Jesse Clayton?"

"Hit the road, head north to Rathdrum. Maybe catch a train. Feel like that could be fun."

"Not tempted to stick around? See how this all turns out?"

He'd thought about it. In the few days he'd been at the ranch, he'd mulled the idea of staying. Bill had offered him steady work as a ranch hand. Said he'd be grateful for the help and that Winona would love it, too. Winona just kept talking of leaving. She had the idea of chasing that dream now and was just waiting for her wound to heal. She was the only reason worth staying and she wasn't even sticking around.

"Nah," Jesse settled with saying. "Besides, what would I even do around here."

"Well, for one, the Squires girl has taken a shine to you." Frank winked as he said it and Jesse could feel himself reddening, "And this town is still in desperate need of a sheriff."

"Oh, you wouldn't want that, Frank."

"Why?"

"We might've killed men together. Hell, you saved my life. But if I put that tin star on, we couldn't be friends. And you'd have to stop cheating at cards."

Frank pointed an accusing finger. "You can't prove that."

They both laughed.

"Goddamn, I'm gonna miss you, Jesse. You take care of yourself." He walked over to Jesse and enclosed him in a tight hug, pulled away and said, "And remember this. You ever find yourself in need, you'll always have friends in Fortune."

"I will, Frank. Thank you."

"Oh, and before you go . . ." Frank reached inside his jacket and pulled out a small knife in a leather sheaf. "It's a boot knife. For the next time you lose your gun."

Jesse took the knife. It was about five inches in length with a smooth, wooden handle. He offered his hand to Frank one last time as he thanked him. The two men shook, this time without trying to crush bones.

"You'll want this as well . . ." Frank reached into his jacket pocket and held out a folded wad of dollars. "Your half of the split pot." Jesse took it and nodded his appreciation. Frank waved Jesse on. "Go on, get out of here before we find something else to talk about. Good luck, kid."

"Goodbye, Frank."

∼

He was at the edge of town with nothing but the clothes he was wearing, his Colt and his war bag. Winona was standing in front of him, telling him about how she was going to move to a city, and try and find work in a travelling show or join a theater. She had no idea how any of that worked but she'd figure it out. She at least wanted to try. He listened to the softness of her voice, and he watched her even softer lips move with every word.

"What will you do, Jesse?"

"I'll be sure to look you up in every city."

Winona laughed. He loved to hear it. "No, silly, where will you go?"

"Well. The Foys killed my horse. Luckily, Wilkerson over there. . ." Jesse pointed to Wilkerson sitting atop his wagon, who waved at them. ". . . is on his way to Rathdrum and agreed to take me along for the ride. Works for him, I guess, having a gun on board. After that, I've not really thought about it. Honestly, I'm not sure, Winona."

"Wherever the wind takes you?"

"Maybe," Jesse said. "It might just carry me back here . . . or maybe even back to you."

"I'd like that." Winona smiled.

"I would, too."

A moment passed awkwardly as Jesse sensed an opportunity he didn't take.

He adjusted his hat and said, "Well, I—"

Winona took it instead. She stepped forward, grabbed him by the collar and pressed her lips against his. They were even softer than they looked. He felt drums in his chest and fireworks in his belly. She pulled away after what felt like plenty, yet not enough.

"Better to regret what you did than what you didn't," she said and looked away.

He pulled her close and kissed her and again felt the fireworks and drums. After a moment, she pulled away and looked at him, both hands clutching his coat. Jesse saw that there was something in the way she was regarding him. If he didn't know any better, he'd say there was a glint of mischief in her eyes.

"Jesse," Winona began in a tone that confirmed his suspicion, "I don't suppose there's a chance you could stay one more day, is there?"

Jesse glanced over at Wilkerson, who was now waving at him to come over, and then back at Winona and her impish smile.

"You know . . . I think I just might."

Printed in Great Britain
by Amazon